# A

# VETERANS

# ANTHOLOGY

Featuring
John Patterson
Julie Woodside
Lionel de Maine
John Rosskopf
Marcia Ehinger
Gregg Matson
P.L. Clark
Mark Paxson
Fred Ryan
E.K. Lloyd Williams
Berthold Gambrel

Edited by
Mark Paxson

This is a collection of stories featuring veterans. Many stories are fiction and represent characters, places, and events that are the products of the authors' imaginations. For those stories that are non-fiction, the stories are those of the authors and their loved ones.

*To All Those Who Served*

# A Note

The idea for this anthology originated after an earlier idea failed. What I asked for this anthology were stories that include a veteran. I also hoped that this wouldn't become a relentless hero worship of veterans and instead present veterans in many different forms.

I think that's what I got. There are nonfiction tributes to fathers who served, a couple of futuristic tales, and plenty of stories based on wars we all know about from the history books, and maybe even our own experiences.

I hope you enjoy these stories and that they have done justice to the subject matter.

I'd like to thank the authors who trusted me to put this together and submitted their stories, and also express my appreciation to Marcia Ehinger, who read the manuscript for me after I thought I had caught everything. I had not. I'd also like to thank Karen Phillips for donating her time and art for the cover.

All proceeds beyond costs will go to a charity that benefits veterans.

# Table of Contents

# "There's No Heroes!"
### (John Patterson)

"That's right, John." The Saturday night World War II TV movie ended with Dad's declaration to ten-year-old John. "All the heroes are dead." With that, he got up and went to bed.

When I consider my family origin story, Dad is the man I admire most in the world. He'll always be a hero to me. He was a WWII U.S. Army veteran, enlisted a year before Pearl Harbor. I grew up watching war movies with him, reading books and stories about the war and the enemies. I still watch them, even in retirement. I always picture Dad somewhere in those films. The films try to represent real people. The movies get me to step into mock situations similar to those they were in and parse how they tried to handle them.

I didn't go to Vietnam, nor serve, which upset my parents. "You have to do your duty like Grandpa and your dad." My problem was, I didn't think that war was right. I thought we were being lied to. I wanted everyone back home. Tragically, several guys from my high school did not come back sitting up.

Death and mangling are part of war. That is difficult to grasp. I'm on board with the fact readers may be angry because I didn't serve and that I'm writing here. I'm not arguing with you.

A baby boomer, I grew up thinking serving in the Army was the most honorable thing a man could do. I wanted to go to West Point.

Dad represented the typical man in that war. I learned about him growing up, as we worked for a few years to save our house from landslides, me barely old enough for Little League at the start of our multi-year endeavors, and the oldest of four, then five, kids. I thought I was helping, steadying the wheelbarrow, reheating coffee for him, helping him shovel. I did more each of the following years and he kept sharing stuff about himself, which kept me incredulous.

But those years, those times, that's when Dad discussed things as he looked far off and saw nothing but the past. He, I understand now, was processing his life before and after 1941. Experiences and situations packed his life. Then, in Tiburon, we had a landslide pile on the front of our house. Dad spent a year after work shoveling dried mud and stabilizing the hill in front of our house with rock terraces. No insurance money, no city help, all on his/our own. The following year, we had a bigger slide in the back.

When he took a break from shoveling, after dinner, before sunset, while Mom worked the swing shift as a switchboard operator at San Rafael General Hospital, he'd say a few things while holding a cup of coffee in one hand and a lit cigarette in the other. Listening, I learned about him at the same time I was being brought to church more. His stories made me think more about God, as well as what a childhood and life he'd had.

An early story occurred in the afternoon after watching *Victory at Sea*, a TV documentary about the war in the Pacific. He never wanted to miss that weekend's morning show. "John, climbing down those ropes from the ship to the landing boats isn't as easy as it looks. First, it takes a lot of work to hold on and get your boot on the next rung down. Everything is moving: the ship, the water, and the boat. Everybody climbing down is moving the rope. You can't slip, get your leg on the inside, it gets trapped." He paused. Looked away.

At eight years old, I started hearing these bits. As I did, I wanted to know more about him.

Most of us wouldn't recognize his life. Born in 1917 Wyoming, a place with notoriously cold winters more than half a year long. On January 3, the bottom drawer provided a bed and warmth for the youngest of three children bundled into Grandpa's small brakeman's shack on a railway line. The day his dad came back from WWI in 1918, my grandfather's best friend returned the borrowed shotgun, which accidentally discharged, severing Grandpa's leg. All the way through the war and what a welcome home. Two years later, Dad's year older brother died from eating gum off the street because he was hungry, per the four-year-old's explanation. It was also the time of the "Spanish Flu" epidemic. Then, Grandma divorced Grandpa. He left Wyoming to mine and live in Idaho. Dad grew up the younger of two with a single mom.

But that isn't what takes my breath away. He's almost a teen when the Great Depression starts. That's true for most of the WWII vets. And it being Wyoming, I don't think there were any dollars around. He told stories of how he and other thick-skinned kids thought they could handle pitching pennies against the wall in Casper alleys, "It was against the law, John." They tried to make money off each other the only place they could find it. They also risked losing what they had. Sometimes, older kids came and took all the pennies, banging some heads along the way. This increased wariness and toughness for a young teen trying to get a couple pennies. Casper's, like other cities', streets sported gangsters too, and Dad, while in high school, got a .22 bullet in the gut from a known drug dealer for coming around the wrong corner at the wrong time.

Dad wasn't a bitter man. He worked harder, in more difficult conditions, all for family, than any man I ever knew. I'm fascinated by his dedication. Tough situations kept coming at him. I grew up hearing that there is a bit of Native American (my parents said Indian) blood in our family. Nobody has any record of this, nor ever makes much of this interesting bit of family lore.

Before his senior year, his mom and the principal met with him at school to do "the best thing for him to finish school." They placed Dad in an "Indian" school and boarding house on the Sioux Reservation. This would be the middle of the Great Depression. His mom, as I grasped it, worked her six ten-hour shifts at the Wigwam Bakery and still had to make sourdough bread at home for her family every day. So, he lived on the Reservation and played football to start his senior year. "It was a little semi-pro, sometimes." He made a big "Ufff!" sound as he explained, grinning a little to himself. "Because they'd bus us to some places that weren't schools. The other guys were a couple years older, folks lined the sidelines, or jail yards, and after the games, each player would get some money on the bus. We laughed a lot." He looked around, seeing through me again, and continued. "We had fun and ignored being bruised, bloodied, and banged up. Nobody cared about us."

******

At nine, I first learned how serious Dad's condition was with a loud crack, waking up in the middle of the night, hearing faint groans. My brother and I were asleep on army surplus cots in the unfinished attic when I heard the unusual sounds.

******

4

It's important to know Dad just before the war. After Dad's senior year of football, he told me, referring to school, "There was nothing there for me, so I left, walked off one evening after the last game."

The more I found out about him, the more I wanted to know. The older I got, the more I learned about reservation schools and boarding houses, the more I wanted to know. Wyoming snow starts by early October. I pieced together that football is over in late November, mid-December sometimes. This guy walks off with the clothes on his back and virtually no money. He somehow ended up on a large cattle ranch, hired and trained as a cowboy, getting boots, hat, saddle, horse, and a rifle.

December 1940, a year before Pearl Harbor, he enlists while in Casper. Probably didn't see any jobs or opportunities coming around. And, as you have surmised, without a high school diploma.

******

After getting him a cup of coffee on a break from working one weekend afternoon, I listened as he sat on a rock. "I want you to do well in school, John. It's better that way. I didn't finish high school." That's when I heard the Reservation story. "I'm good. They have something for guys like me, called a G.E.D. After the war, I went to night school, studied, passed the test. It's like graduating. I want you to do it the other way."

******

I've read about our country before the war. Before WWII, most Americans lived in rural situations. And less than half the kids graduated from high school. After Pearl Harbor, he was stationed at Forts Cronkite and Baker just

a couple miles north of Sausalito, itself just across the
Golden Gate Bridge from San Francisco.

******

"We were the first ones there, and they had us dig
holes. That's where we slept. And they had us dig more
holes. More guys came, we dug more holes. I was a
sergeant on a machine gun crew. And there'd be fights in
the holes, and I'd get busted back to private. That
happened a few times. But I was always in charge of the
machine gun."

That night, lying on my cot, looking up at the
bottom sides of the shingles, I thought a lot about Dad. I
tried to picture the changes he went through during the
Depression. The reservation school, a cowboy, the army,
Pearl Harbor, stationed in the San Francisco Bay Area,
and now he's in charge of a machine gun. Did he bring the
machine guns from Wyoming? If they didn't have places
for him to sleep, if he's digging holes, they probably didn't
have a bunch of new ones, so they brought what they had.
Because its Wyoming, they had old WW I machine guns.
Yeah.

But he doesn't know anything about war. He's
probably seen newspaper pictures and news reels of Pearl
Harbor and Europe. It's a surprise war. Nice young men,
like at Pearl Harbor. They see something different.
They're not thinking to shoot first. Sailors shot back after
the enemy fired. How do you prepare for shooting, and
shooting first is a must in those situations, when there's
no shooting war around? If you went to Pearl Harbor,
then you were ready to shoot!

The next night after school, dinner, and back to the
rocks and dirt.

Another break from shovel and dump.

"We're told, 'Be ready. You're here to keep them away.' Thought we'd see planes." He shrugs. "Then one night, we barely see a silhouette on the water. It's not a ship! Get it. We fire and immediately white tracers are coming, whiz right by us. Tat-a-tat-tats fill the air. Our holes to their silhouette, their silhouettes to our holes." He paused. "Both sides trying to get their tracers to hit the start of the tracers coming at them."

They'd heard about Pearl Harbor. None of them had seen any enemy planes, boats, anything being close to the mainland. They were on guard, just in case. Then, in the middle of another boring night, an instant machine gun fight. Without any warning, it must have been terrifying.

"And then the silhouette was gone. In the morning, we received confirmation. None of our ships were out there. We were told there was some oily brown cloth and a couple of pieces of wood from small wooden boxes floating in that area. We're not supposed to talk about it, ever."

I've read a few things online over the last couple of years that gave me chills. I've told a few friends who have scoffed. But I've learned that Japanese subs sailed off the west coast in a few places, including firing on oil storage tanks in Santa Barbara. Some subs held planes on their decks that would take off and drop incendiary devices on Oregon forests, trying to start fires and divert resources. I've also read that one night, anti-aircraft batteries over Los Angeles fired off hundreds of rounds.

At other times, watching *Victory at Sea*, he'd see maps on the TV and say, "That's where that is!"

Our troops came from this country, sailed on transports for a few weeks, climbed down rope ladders, and went ashore to war.

"The Marquesas Islands. That's the most beautiful place in the world."

******

"John, help! HELP!"
Is that Mom screaming?

******

Another time we're watching *Victory at Sea*.
"John, on those ropes, you have to be quick. Guys are being rushed down behind you. You can't wait. You gotta judge your jump to the boats. They're going up and down and swinging in close to the ship. If you go too low..." he turns and looks away, "Well, you can't, not everyone jumps into the boats, but you've got to go."

******

That's Mom!
It's completely dark. I jumped up and bounded down the stairs. My breathing and gasping grabbed and tightened the back of my mouth. I heard heavy sounds of scraping, and squeaking, gurgling, gasps, and "uuhs", some short, some long. I opened the door at the bottom of the stairs.

Light was spilling into the front room from the hall. I looked at the front door. It was closed. My eyes quickly scanned to the hall. The light from the bathroom flooded the hall. The uninterrupted noises came from the bathroom. I heard Mom yell my name. I turned and saw the bathroom door set at a sharp angle, broken off the bottom hinge, the bottom of the door halfway blocking the hall. I plunged into the hallway. The door, sprinkled with blood splotches, barely hung by two partially attached screws protruding from the middle hinge.

"John" pierced my ears with a loud, shrieking sound. I turned right into the bathroom. I saw Dad's back bent over the bathtub, his arms extended in front of him. I jumped up beside him. His hands were around Mom's neck. She was upside down in the bathtub, blood splotched face and arms, trying to push his arms off.

"Dad, DAAAAddd!!!, STOP!" I yelled as I threw my arms out and grabbed at his right arm, crawling over the toilet seat, it giving way and sliding off behind me as my knee crashed into the toilet bowl. Oooooph!

Things happened simultaneously. A wild-eyed Dad turned and looked at me square in the eye, from two inches away, something that had never occurred, and he yelled, "What?" It terrified me. How mad at me will he be?

At the same time, Mom yelled, "He's trying to kill me again!" She gasped. His hands are still on her neck, but he isn't bearing down on her. I'm pulling his right arm. "He thinks I'm a Jap," she's pushing the same arm I'm pulling, "that I'm, uugll, trying to kill him."

I hear this. Can that be possible? Can that happen?

While they're yelling at me, my fallen knee in the toilet finishes crashing to the bottom of the bowl. I lose my balance, while ever so instantly thinking about Mom's statement, and my descent into the toilet causes my left knee to bend out, hitting Dad under the armpit.

He finishes yelling, "Yarraaaghh!" while turning back to me and jumps up, knocking my back against the top of the toilet, staring at me in disbelief. I picture the blue bruise coming across my back. He's got a quizzical look on his face.

More yelling, it's all so loud and quick. "Get him out of here, John. He doesn't know what he's doing!" I turn to Mom. Her white nightgown streaked with red rivers of blood that's gushed from her face and her nose. Each tub squeak and Mom groan accompanies her trying to sit up and get out of the tub. "Go, goooo!" She implores in her yells.

I climb up and push Dad towards the door so I can stand, then step by him, grabbing his hand. I pull him to the front room as Dave walks downstairs. Looking back, I see Mom is wobbling from the hallway, dripping blood streams over her frayed and now torn gown. Seeing her this way makes things much worse. I take in her red neck as she yells hoarsely.

"Get your bat! Nowww! Knock him out, he's gonna kill me." He turns to her with a meanness in his face I hadn't seen and couldn't believe was real. She's louder and gruffer, "Goooooo!"

I push him back towards the fireplace and run upstairs. I reach and grab the bat on the floor without going all the way to the top of the stairs and again bound down, with more need and confidence in my steps and more fear, as I now have a bat I don't want to fall on. I'm afraid of tumbling down, until I get to the bottom, proud I could do two stairs at a time, wondering how I did it. *What am I going to do?* My head screams at me.

"Hurry, John!" Followed by "Noooo, Pat!" Dad's new nickname from work. He'd explained earlier that after the war a lot of men called each other by their last name.

I get downstairs as he's stepping towards Mom in the hall. I jump in front of him, yelling, "Daaaaad!"

He looks quizzically at me again. I grab his hand and yank him towards the fireplace.

"Don't wait, do it John!" Mom implores.

I bring my bat back and swing. A knock at the door. Mom turns and steps towards it. It's the middle of the night. *Are we at war?*

Dad's dropping to his knees. I've started to swing when I turn towards the front door…. What do I do? And Mom had said, "Again. He's trying to kill me again." Towards the end of my swing I look back and see cops are at the door! He's now laying out flat on the floor, face down.

What did I do? Did I feel I hit anything with the bat?

******

Sunday morning, I'm helping Mom fix pancakes while Dad's gone to the hardware store.

I learned because he'd had a few drinks the night before and or because it was a dream, he might not remember it. He didn't act like anything unusual had occurred. Monday, after school, helping Mom fix dinner for when Dad got home and before she left for work, she told me more. Mom said he'd passed out. Maybe I didn't hit him? The cops felt she'd be safe. He slept on the floor all night.

Mom leaned over to me while I'm standing on a chair working at the kitchen sink. "John, this happened once before."

I look at her. Neither of us moves our eyes, locked on each other, only a spatula's length apart.

She continued in her hushed tones. "It happened when we lived in Santa Barbara."

"When did you live there? Where's that?"

"Just after the war. It's a beautiful area. This is before your time."

"So, …."

"Santa Barbara, it's on the southern coast of California. Yeah, it was bad. I had to call the Shore Patrol and got them involved."

11

"You called Shore Patrol?"

"Your Dad needed to go to a hospital. It was hard for him in the war."

"Umm. Are you OK?"

"Yea. It's awful. We're hoping it'll pass."

"He said nothing? He doesn't act like he has any thoughts about me and the bat."

"No, no, John. He doesn't. He doesn't even remember what happened. No, he doesn't even know about it. Not you, the bat, the cops, none of it. I told him we slipped and broke the door, so
yesterday he was trying to fix it."

I'm staring. "Umm."

"I had wiped most of the blood off. I told him I bumped my nose."

"He doesn't know anything?"

She's shaking her head back and forth. "I'm gonna talk to him some, this weekend, soon, about relaxing, getting more sleep, talking about things he thinks about."

"Hospital, geez, what was that like?"

"I don't really know. They took him to Denver for that."

"Geez Mom!"

"Yeah, it was for most of a year. But the timing worked out. After you were born, I took the train. He was so excited to see you. And then we took the train north to Casper, and I met his mom and she saw you."

******

From that exchange, I learned the other incident occurred nine years earlier. I knew my parents were under tremendous pressure, having four kids, with him rising at 5 am to go to work in a meat packing plant, her working the night shift on a switchboard after he got home. That's how they handled childcare and shared one car. And moving dirt to save the house. I grew up knowing everything is for family, everything.

Decades later, when I heard the oil storage tanks came under attack from Japanese submarines, I finally understood why the Shore Patrol was in Santa Barbara.

The following year, after we removed the hillside from the front of our house, another landslide took away much of the back yard and left a few feet of the garage hanging over a fifteen-foot drop. We spent a couple of years filling that hole. There was no help of any type. During those years of relocating dump truck loads of rock and dirt from our driveway to the huge deprivation behind the house, there were more stories when Dad took coffee and cigarette breaks on the weekends and evenings. I was ten when I heard, in parts over a few episodes of telling, the worst story I've ever heard.

******

"John, there are some things that, after they're done, they're hard to be done with." He drank a bit of coffee. He was looking up. "There was so much fighting. No one knew anybody or anything. We were all strangers. Everyone was afraid, but wouldn't say it. No one knew when it would end. No one knew who would win. Like I said, I was sergeant, busted back to private, and back to sergeant again, a few times. But I stayed the machine gunner."

We worked on the rocks every night that week. I heard the rest of his story.

Monday: "In some gun fights, the barrels got so hot they melted and you had to change them, sometimes with your bare hands. You'd get blistered hands. You're scared,

13

thinking it'll end while you're changing, and then, when you're done, you jump right back to shooting.

Tuesday: Shovel, push wheelbarrow, dump, an hour later, a break. "After one of our landings, we went into the jungle, and later, more of our guys came after a battle started." He pauses, sets the cup down, lights another cigarette.

"It was so hot, always hungry and thirsty. You couldn't see much. Some islands are beautiful, like the Marquesas. Other places are terrifying jungles with bugs and swamps. You can't see. You can hardly walk, carrying a heavy gun, ammunition, and your rifle on your back."

Wednesday: "One battle," He never looked at me while he recounted these stories. He looked past me. "They just kept coming. They're the fiercest, most dedicated fighters.... They outnumbered us three, four, five, who knows, to one...." He stops looking past me and hands me his empty cup to put on the porch. "Let's just do a couple more barrow loads, OK?"

That question that was a statement.

Thursday: A long coffee break. "No matter how many we killed, they kept coming.... The fighting kept going, guys getting ammo from guns not being used because.... They kept coming.... At the end.... All over the ground and the water.... They outnumbered us by so many.... Fewer and fewer shots around me.... Metal scraping, groans.... Both sides... " He stood up quicker than usual. "Thanks for the coffee, John. Let's go in!"

Friday night. "Let's just do a little tonight, John." He busted some rocks, loaded a wheelbarrow. I wheeled, busted, the sledgehammer so heavy; he wheeled, dumped. A few more loads. He seemed troubled tonight, anxious. Asked me to get him some coffee. He said he wanted to knock off early, take it easy, stay up to see Mom.

He sat on a low rock. I handed the coffee to him. He looked at me for a few seconds and then took out a cigarette and lit it. "Yeah, I was sayin', bayonet fighting.... Only.... No shots.... None from any direction...." He was talking slower. "Over. Not dark. I was.... was the only one.... Yeah, the only one, uh...." Silence. "Everyone," whispering. "Everyone else.... Hmm...." His head is turning, as if looking around. It's like he's looking at the ground all around him. "Was the only one...." Silence. "Yeah, so I couldn't tell which way we came from... Or if more were going to charge us...." Longer pause. "Uhmmm, me...." Now the longest pause as he finishes looking around the ground and looks through me again. "It was three days before they found me."

We sat together in silence for minutes and then he went in while I put the tools away. His "three days" haunts me.

******

Later, I learned malaria almost killed him. He came back to the states in a hospital ship. Not every sick G.I. came back that way. Not every guy that struggled with PTSD ("shell shock") got hospitalized a couple years after the war. Not everyone hospitalized with a non-physical wound was hospitalized for more than half a year.

There's no going back from hearing this. I've lived my entire life being outraged at what my parents had to endure after that service on his part. After the war, he could only support Mom and himself in San Francisco with the available work. He hauled ice blocks from a cart he loaded during pre-dawn hours. He used tongs to carry the blocks on a leather shoulder wrap up flights of Victorian stairs to people's ice boxes.

For almost thirty years after the war, he lived the unabated daily pressure of two working parents raising six children. They put up with a lot of abuse to keep their relatively low-paying jobs. He kept used cars running, with little sick pay and minimal vacations. While living on the San Francisco Peninsula, he drove to Lake Tahoe, a gorgeous location, on the weekends, and built a home he otherwise couldn't afford. After having the early morning butcher experience during some snowy winters, they moved back to the peninsula. After Mom passed away, needing a change and a more modest home, he built another home in the foothills. He'd saved our home in Tiburon from two different landslides over three years of shoveling after work. He lived proudly, albeit modestly, having taken another low paying full-time job to supplement inadequate social security and his butcher's pension. He always put in the extra effort to get more than he could afford to pay for. He passed in 1999. He knew what he'd done in his life, and what he'd done some fifty plus years earlier stopping the enemy advance. He also knew that no one else knew. He wasn't a feted hero.

"Taps," a twenty-four-note bugled tribute developed in 1862, honors veterans at their last service. The military might provide a bugler. Most funeral directors can assist in this process. If no military bugler is located, two organizations provide a bugler: Taps for Veterans and Bugles Across America. It is okay for a civilian to play taps at a veteran's funeral. In uniform, you may salute if you feel it is appropriate. If you have a cap, remove it during "Taps." You might look down, or you may look up, but please, say "Thank you."

## About John Patterson

As a kid, John Patterson was fascinated with how hard his parents worked and how difficult their situations were. He always wanted people to know about his dad's life. He inspired John to shoulder tough times.

John worked kid jobs. Then he held a variety of service, retail, and blue-collar gigs thru college, and heavy blue-collar work for almost a decade after, including welding in shipyards. After finishing law school in two and a half years, including a clerking internship at the California Supreme Court, he practiced law in Federal and California courts for almost twenty years.

Then he switched careers and went into public secondary education and administration for almost twenty years. He primarily taught Algebra, Geometry, as well as Economics and English, before retiring. As an administrator, he managed a federal grant at a challenged high school. He's served on five boards and hosts Open Readings, which he started four years ago.

He's always wanted people to look closer at those who work very hard with comparatively smaller rewards. He's currently working on a childhood memoir. When not writing, seeing family, gardening, or travelling, he tells true stories. He is screening for beta readers.

Contact: 2johnpatterson@gmail.com

# Quan Loi: Rocket City
### (Julie Woodside)

The fourth night the rat comes, he's ready.

That afternoon, sweating in the humid shade, he'd taken a shell from his M-16 and, holding it carefully vertical to preserve the precious gunpowder within, eased the copper jacketed 5.56mm round from its casing. Taking his also precious army-issued bar of soap, he'd gently worked it down onto the top of the casing, leaving – yes, a hole in his soap, but also a "soap bullet" in the shell, which will be safer for himself in the coffin-sized space where the execution will take place.

He's practiced aiming in the daylight at the dab of army-issue peanut butter he's smeared near his right foot on the sandbags lining his hole. Later, he will need to make the same shot in the dark. The space is too small to get the enticing peanut butter far from where his foot will be.

"Bang!" he whispers each time. Rounds are too dear to waste on practice.

Over his head, the red dirt of this part of Vietnam. Plus, perforated steel plates liberated from elsewhere in camp and piled with a dozen layers of sandbags. Just feet away, his bunkmates sleep in the wooden hooch. He'd slept in there, too, in his assigned corner bunk, until five nights ago – his second night in this huge, cleared-of-jungle camp nicknamed Rocket City, the name earned by the frequency of rocket mortars arriving at night, sounding like giant monsters walking into and angrily stomping across the compound.

That night when the mortars started arriving and he'd learned the meaning of the nickname, he'd fled with his hooch-mates to the nearest underground, reinforced bunker. His wounds were minor enough to be able to help giving first aid to those who'd been less lucky. When the morning brought silence from the jungle, he'd returned to his hooch to find daylight coming through the roof over his bunk and a fist-sized hole in his pillow.

By that night, he'd designed and built his own sleeping bunker, cutting a crawl space through the bottom of the hooch wall, digging a cot-sized hole in the red dirt with an army-issue shovel, and fortifying it. This way he can muster with his mates, but sleep better in his one-man dirt-and- steel-and-sand-bag cave.

Except for the rat.

It's come every night, its big feet and feral smell traveling the length of his body time and again.

In a coffin-sized hole, a rat has a large presence, and it's not welcome. The young man has little enough he can control in this mixed-up insane world he's been assigned to. But he can improve his chances of living through the night, and he can do something about a stinky, sleep-stealing rat.

Around midnight he senses it sneaking in. Feels it race across his shoulders in the dark, dart down his left side, then cross his ankles. He hears it sniffing deeply at the peanut butter, the scrape of teeth on the sandbag. "Bang!" he whispers as he pulls the trigger, his word lost in the real bang. His ears reverberate in spite of the cotton he'd swiped from a first aid kit he's stuffed into them.

Quan Loi wasn't his first assignment. He's been in this jungle long enough that sleeping with the corpse at the foot of his cot doesn't bother him. He can take it out in the morning, when it's light and no surprise mortars might come raining out of the sky. At least tonight, there are no monsters walking above his head or in his bunker.

He pulls the cotton out of his ears, then thinks better of it and puts it back in. He scrunches his pillow under his head and dreams of home. He's safe again. For now.

# About Julie Woodside

I wrote the story, Quan Loi: Rocket City after hearing the true-life vignette from a friend. He'd told it in about four sentences after hearing I'd once had a pet rat. His way of sharing rat tales, I guess. Just a day or two later I saw a five-hundred word contest and wrote a 500-word version. I liked the tight confines of five hundred words, similar to the tight confines of the bunker my friend had dug himself to improve his chances of living through any given night.

When I shared the story I'd written with him, my friend added several details he'd felt were important, and also gave me the name of Quan Loi, which I could then research to find images to give myself a better feel for the hellish place he'd spent time as a new recruit to the war. I allowed the extra details to swell the story to 624 words, but resisted the urge to keep adding to it. I still want it centered on the execution of the rat to stand in for the massive amount of senseless killing taking place around the hole our nameless hero has dug in the dirt. The idea of sleeping soundly with a freshly blown up rat carcass only inches from him seems to capture for me the essence of the craziness of the whole situation. "Better it than me," as my friend summed it up.

It's the only 'war story' in my collection of writing so far. I have in my head some true stories from my father that will get written at some point, but I haven't found the angle for them yet. His stories tended to be light on details or emotions, but the longer it's been since his passing the more I'm willing to add 'creative' details to turn them into stories.

Many of my stories started as something true for someone. A news story, a personal anecdote from a friend or stranger, a snatch of overheard conversation. I enjoy fleshing them out and trying to answer some of the questions left by hearing something out of context or time. I strive for authentic emotions by adding whatever details seem to create the sense I had when hearing it from the person who lived it.

"It's the toughest job I've ever had" was recently said by a woman running a Laundromat, for example. What would make that job so difficult? What kinds of people or duties would pile up for her? What other jobs has she had to compare it to? These are fun to ruminate on and hopefully a story emerges that will carry that sense of intrigue I had on hearing it.

If you want to read more from me, you'll have a hard time finding it. I've a poem in an anthology on Marriage from Pure Slush in Australia; an anthology of Short Stories out of Bristol, England; two (or is it three?) in lit journals that are now out of print. But hit me up at my email Juwoodside@aol.com and I'll gladly send you something – I've got stories as short as 100 words and as long as 10,000, just tell me how long you want and I'll gladly oblige. Meanwhile, thank you for reading this one, and I wish you a great life full of good stories.

# Something Moved
### (Lionel de Maine)

I was hiding from the war when Brian peered into the officers' mess. Sunlight burned the edge of his silhouette to a crisp and flecks of dust floated off his uniform. I wanted to pity him and invite him in out of the heat, but I also wanted to tell him to bugger off, treat him as others did. People disliked Brian because he tried to buy friendship with the things he pilfered. "Spoils of war," he would say, his eyes darting like a frightened weasel's. "Been with us since the Crusaders conquered Constantinople." He seemed to like the sound of the alliteration.

His offerings to me had included an "especially light sleeping bag," a "hardly used car tire," and five gallons of "petrol worth its weight in gold." Fuel was rationed in Rhodesia and my monthly ration card seldom lasted a month, so the petrol pushed me close to accepting his bribe, but I stopped myself. "Next time you offer me stolen petrol," I said, angry more at myself than at him, "I'll make sure you're fucking charged with stealing government property." When the look of surprise had fallen from his face, he saluted and skulked away. In his over-starched uniform, he looked like a beetle poking its ginger head from an oversized shell.

"I have something for you," he called, "outside—in the truck."

The last thing I wanted was to go outside. The sun was so harsh that its rays seemed to strip the texture from everything. The giant Baobab trees, upside-down trees, that populated the area merged into the brittle haze of heat that touched the horizon. Scattered rocks and boulders seemed to shimmer over sand that was too hot to touch.

"Come on, come on." Brian stalked uninvited into the room.

Off to my right the refrigerator clanked into life and began to whine. The bottle of beer on the table before me was almost full and coated with an uneven layer of condensation. This was my second beer and I had been looking forward to finishing it in peace. It was a popular lager that we called Shumba, lion in the Shona language. I stroked the bottle with a finger and watched a small puddle of water form on the tabletop. The glass was cool to the touch.

"You'll like my surprise." He grabbed my arm.

I shrugged free. He paused for a moment, his mouth chewing on indecision, before he placed his hand on my shoulder. His touch annoyed me, but I killed the urge to smack his hand away as I realized that he was brimming with genuine excitement, something out of character for Brian. He could keep a poker face while stretching the truth to comic proportions or allow nasty remarks to bring him almost to tears, but only if it served his purpose. To avoid the wrath of officers, he traded on the camaraderie inherent between whites in Africa. Bartering was his business and he prided himself on staying calm.

"Come on." He yanked at my sleeve again. "See for yourself."

"Bugger off Brian—you're as irritating as a fucking mosquito."

He plopped into a chair beside me with a tired sigh. "The truck's right outside."

"What have you stolen this time?" I said, ready for the discussion to end.

He tightened his mouth with a touch of assumed anger. "What have I stolen?"

"I warned you once before about stealing and selling petrol."

"Sir," he said, excitement spilling into his voice, "this is not petrol—it's much better."

"Be careful Brian—there's space in the detention barracks for you."

"This is beautiful," he said. "Something special. Not government property."

He stretched out his legs as though he belonged in the officers' mess, wriggled his spine into the crook of the chair and sighed again, this time with pleasure. Before I could tell him not to get too comfortable, the refrigerator rattled to life again and sent his eyes roving from my beer bottle to the refrigerator and back to my beer bottle.

"Howze about offering me a nice cold Shumba?"

"No," I said. "Let's see what you've scrounged today."

He dashed ahead of me, glancing over his shoulder every few seconds to make sure I was not lagging too far behind. The truck was parked in the imagined shade of an upside-down tree, its branches twisted and knotted like roots. Scabs of gray bark flaked from a trunk five feet across and twice as tall. He swung the passenger door open and flipped the seat forward. The cab smelled of grease and plastic hot enough to blister a person's skin. He dug a brown bag from under some sacking.

"Take it," he said. "It's especially for you."

He gripped the bag in both hands and offered it to me. Ginger hair curled along the tops of his fingers. I was curious now and took the package, but he clung to it so tenaciously that I almost had to jerk it from his grasp. The bag contained a heavy glass jar—the wide-mouthed kind farmwives used to preserve fruit and jam—the worn cap visible inside the paper, the green letters faded on metal shiny from frequent handling.

My mother had preserved jam in jars with screw caps as worn as this one. Her blackberry jam was my favorite, but now I remembered something else. One day, while bottling peaches, she told me that I was her oldest child only because she had miscarried during her first pregnancy. By rights, she said, you should have a big sister. She turned away then, but not quickly enough to stop me seeing her tears. Thinking to comfort her, I went to hug her and, in the process, knocked a bottle of peaches onto the floor where it shattered and sent slivers of glass sliding over the linoleum. That was the last time we ever spoke of the big sister who might have been.

I squeezed the jar tightly, not wanting to drop and ruin the jam or preserved fruit it contained.

"Thanks," I said. "I'll donate this to the officer's mess."

While he latched the seat into place, I strolled across the baked sand, wondering why he'd given me jam and recalled my mother's blackberry jam spooned onto warm bread dripping with butter.

On our farm, Monday afternoons were set aside for baking, and on Monday nights my brother and I gorged on hot bread, ignoring my mother's request that we leave some for the rest of the week. I entered the mess with the taste of blackberry jam filling my mouth. My eyes were still adjusting to the gloom when Brian flicked on the light and strode towards the table.

"Turn the light off," I ordered. "I like the darkness in here."

He sat down at the table without turning the light off.

"Go on—open the bottle," he said. "It's not jam like you think."

"What do you want from me, Brian—why are you giving me this?"

"Because you're superstitious," he smiled, "I'm giving it to you for good luck."

"Luck," I said. "Luck has fuck all to do with this war." But I was lying. For months I had sensed death creeping closer and had come to believe that only luck was keeping me alive. My job was installing and inspecting radios, mostly in remote bases reachable only over dirt roads that were often mined or chosen for ambushes. Only a week earlier the truck driving on my tail had detonated a land mine. I had had to pull the body of a colleague from the wreckage. I no longer doubted that somewhere on one of these roads there was a bullet or a landmine or a rocket carrying my name.

"Bullshit," said Brian. "You should listen to yourself talk sometimes."

"I don't need luck." I sighed wearily. "What I need is peace and quiet."

For a second, I thought of chasing Brian away, but he would argue until he had cajoled me into opening the package, so I grabbed the jam and ripped the paper off the bottle. It smelled faintly of formaldehyde and was filled with a murky gray liquid. The thought that it was Kachasu, a potent, home-brewed spirit, flashed through my mind. It was easy to believe that Brian drank Kachasu; it had a reputation of destroying brain cells and causing bizarre behavior. He watched me closely. There were scratches that looked like writing on the cap and on the side of the jar there was a label covered with spidery blue ink. I could decipher neither so I turned the bottle over in my hands. Brian swallowed a mouthful of my beer and wiped his mouth with his hand. A pocket of trapped air formed a bubble against the glass as I rotated the bottle and peered into the dusky liquid. Suspended in the liquid, like an astronaut curled up in a space capsule, was a fetus.

The formaldehyde had turned its edges gray, but its features were easy to see when it settled against the glass. On the small hands, fingernails were visible and on its head the nub of a nose already had nostrils. Two bulges above the nose were eyes covered with eyelids and beneath the nose was a swollen upper lip that the formaldehyde seemed to have turned soft and spongy.

"Where the fucking hell did you get this?"

"Well," asked Brian, his voice loud with anticipation, "what do you think?"

A tentative smile touched his face. The heat had squeezed the moisture from his skin and blood oozed from cracks in the corners of his mouth. He had nicked his face below his right sideburn when he shaved, but he had missed a patch of ginger beard on his right cheek. He took another swig of my beer and the ginger stubble on his Adam's apple twitched as he swallowed. The smile hovering on his face triggered a prickle of anger inside me. Suddenly I had an urge to swat him, backhanded, across the patch of unshaved beard on his cheek.

"Put my fucking beer down—."

The bottle knocked sharply against the tabletop.

"Where the fucking hell did you find this?"

"We visited that mission that terrs attacked last week. They forced everyone out of the school and the hospital and then shot the place to pieces. The locals looted it before we got— "

"Chisumbanje?" I interjected. For some time, I had wanted to visit the mission.

"— there the floor was covered with broken bottles and spilled medicine. The jar was on a shelf.

Maybe the terrs were afraid of the fetus because they thought the ancestors had refused to accept its spirit. Something like that anyway."

I spun the jar and watched the fetus bob and swirl. As best as I could see through the murk the fetus was female, a young woman who would have earned her father lobola—a bride price traditionally paid in money or cattle—when she married. The lobola was only refundable if the woman later proved to be barren.

"And your plan is to trade her like petrol or a sleeping bag?"

"No Sir," he said, pleased with himself. "I rescued this baby especially for you."

"You're a typical bloody townie—so bloody ignorant about spirits."

I had garnered the little knowledge I possessed about spirits during a childhood spent on my father's farm. One day, I found a bottle hidden in a tree stump and unscrewed the cap.

"Stop," yelled a laborer, "that is special medicine." He rushed at me, his unlaced boots slapping his shins, snatched the bottle from my grasp and shoved it into his coverall pocket. When pressed, he explained that the medicine would appease an ngozi who was making his joints ache. I asked what an ngozi was. Women who were murdered or died childless became ngozi unless special burial rituals were performed to prevent their spirits wandering the earth.

"Yeah," I said. "This fetus is harboring a malicious spirit."

"That fetus will bring you good luck," said Brian. "I was going to leave it behind but at the last minute I grabbed it and stuffed it into a bag. I wasn't sure what to do with it but then I remembered your cockamamie theory—the one about you being a cat with nine lives." He held his blue-green eyes steady. "Remember?"

I leaned my chair onto two legs. "And I still have six lives to go."

"Six lives aren't enough," he said. "Bullets don't discriminate."

"Thanks for the reminder," I said. "But cats are tough creatures."

"Do you know why this fetus will bring you luck?"

I drank some beer, relishing the faint taste of hops on my tongue.

He answered his own question. "One life taken so that another can be spared."

"John three sixteen," I said reflexively. Brian looked confused.

My response reminded me of my old Sunday school teacher, Father Armstrong. Only on rare occasions did I grasp the meaning of his lessons. As an incentive for learning this verse, which I had struggled to recite correctly, he offered me two shillings and sixpence. The words flowed easily as I recited it for Brian's benefit. "For God so loved the world that he gave his only begotten Son, that whosoever believeth in him should not perish, but have everlasting life."

"Make up your mind," said Brian, "do you want the fetus or not?"

"Yes," I said, "We need all the help we can get in this damn war."

"You know," he said, "some of the blokes want this as a war souvenir."

"I wonder how this baby came to be preserved in a bottle?"

"Who knows?" He stood up to leave, but hesitated, thought for a moment as though unsatisfied with his own answer, and then speculated, "A peasant woman with a bunch of kids visits the mission doctor. She can't feed them. She's pregnant. He aborts the baby and keeps the fetus for teaching or something."

With that, he grabbed my beer, drank deeply, put it down and then walked to the door. The door swung open on screeching hinges and the camp stray, an overweight tabby, darted into the mess. Grass and spiked seeds clung to its fur. Brian swung his boot at the cat but missed. The stray's ability to survive had sparked the notion of my nine lives.

"I'm visiting Zulu Five tomorrow," I called. "Do you want to come along?"

"No thanks," said Brian, a silhouette in the doorframe. "That road is too dangerous for me."

"Consider the request a direct order then—you will escort me."

The trip would be no different from hundreds of others I'd made.

"Sorry Sir," he said, "I have too many things to do tomorrow."

"Do you want to be charged with insubordination?"

While I waited for Brian to respond—to disobey my order—the refrigerator rattled awake again and began to whine. We both knew that insubordination was a serious charge and his gaze moved from the fetus to my face and back to the fetus. Disappointment clouded his face.

"I've been on worse roads," he said, shrugging. "When are we leaving?"

"Eight hundred sharp. Johnny will be driving the Puma."

"I like Johnny--isn't he the Greek who just got married?"

"That's him," I said, adding in a friendly tone, "His wife is expecting any day now."

The door slammed behind Brian, leaving me alone with my thoughts, the half-empty bottle of warming beer and the fetus. I peered into the jar and saw a mission doctor in a shabby office, a kindly man like Father Armstrong. Patients queued outside. A woman in a washed-away dress that smelled of carbolic soap pushed the door open. Something moved in her womb as she shuffled into the office. The doctor understood that the war promised only hunger and starvation for her unborn child. Brian had understood that too. My eyes pulled the fetus into focus.

"To put the spirits to rest," I promised, "I'll bury you properly on my father's farm."

Next morning, I left the fetus on a shelf in the wooden shack that served as my quarters. I wanted to lock the fetus—it seemed wrong to call it a lucky charm—away but the only furniture in the hut was a bed frame, a thin felt mattress and my sleeping bag. The prefabricated walls, rough unfinished timber, were bolted to a slab of concrete. The latch on the door was broken. A previous tenant had hammered long nails into the walls to hang clothes from and had built a shelf for books or personal effects. I stood the jar behind my electric razor, deodorant, toothbrush and toothpaste. A thief would steal the razor, not the fetus, I thought.

The sun had already heated the trucks when I got to them. Johnny climbed into the Puma's steel cab through a hatch on top of the vehicle. He left the windows, two holes cut through the steel, open for fresh air, and peered through the two-inch-thick armored glass of the windshield. I climbed onto the Puma and stuck my head through one of the cab's windows. The beginning of black stubble adorned Johnny's face, pressing into a dense shadow around his chin. He'd shaved only as far as his collar bones. Thick hair crawled over his forearms and the tops of his fingers. Light glinted from the gold band on his right hand.

"Howzit?" I asked in greeting.

"It's going to be a scorcher today," responded Johnny.

"Make sure you close your window shutters," I said. "The road's dangerous."

"Hell no," he said, "that will make it hot as hades in this cab."

I did not challenge him. Despite being targets, few drivers closed the shutters.

"Better check your tank," he said. "Brian has probably siphoned it."

"Brian's not a bad type," I said loudly. "And he's handy with a rifle."

Johnny's brow furrowed into a question: what was I saying?

"He's sitting right behind you," I said. "He's in charge of your escort."

Johnny started to cuss, but I ignored him and hauled myself into the Puma's bed, a long steel box with sloped sides. Troopies sat facing outwards on steel benches in the middle of it, only their heads and shoulders exposed. A radio operator, a young black man, perched near the rear of the truck, a swaying whip-antenna protruding from the radio strapped to his back. His uniform hadn't faded with washing yet. "Bring the radio to me immediately if anything happens," I told him. "Where's the first aid kit?"

Usually, I left it on the escort truck, but a sense of premonition warned me to take it today. A white troopie dragged a green canvas bag from under the bench and handed it to me. He looked too young to be a soldier.

"I hope we don't need this today," he said a little nervously.

"We won't," I said. "I'm not planning on dying. How about you?"

"Let the bastards try," he said. "I'm more than ready for them."

A grizzled black soldier laughed. Pinned to his camouflage jacket were six medals in two rows. His combat boots flexed easily, softened by wear and tear. A sheen of oil glistened on his rifle. He rubbed the barrel with his index finger and then examined it for dirt.

Brian sat slouched down behind the cab, his rifle propped on the armored rim of the truck's bed. He'd taped a spare magazine, upside down, to the one clipped into his weapon. He'd missed shaving the ginger patch of hair on his cheek again. Maybe he was missing it on purpose.

"Sir," he grinned, "I'll look after this bunch if anything happens."

"We'll stop at Chisumbanje," I said, "if we have time on the way back."

"Why?" He looked annoyed. "There's nothing left to see there."

"I want to see the church," I said, deciding not to explain why.

Weeks before I'd wandered into a mission church up north. Beautifully painted murals adorned its thick walls. A brave priest had added a heavy lock to the trapdoor into the bell tower to prevent snipers accessing it. The church was cool and dark and smelled vaguely of incense, an island of peacefulness in countryside torn by war, so I had laid my rifle down on a rough-hewn pew and rested there for half an hour. I felt rested and calm when I left the church.

"I don't care much for churches," said Brian. "They're usually empty."

"Nothing to—" I stopped myself before I said pillage.

I jumped off the Puma and walked to my Kudu, a top-heavy armored vehicle built on a Toyota Land Cruiser chassis and shaped like a steel bellows turned on end to deflect bullets and rockets, which sometimes melted through their armor anyway. It was a nightmare to drive. I tossed the canvas first-aid bag behind my seat, steel lined with carpeting.

"Ready?" I asked three black soldiers already seated in the Kudu.

"We are ready," they chorused happily. I hoped they were good shots.

Last season's rains had left the road to Zulu Five rough and furrowed. The Kudu rattled, lurched and filled with dust. My sweaty hands turned the dust on the steering wheel into a slippery skin of mud. The taste of sand worked into my mouth. An hour into the journey the road dropped sharply toward a crumbling concrete bridge in the bed of a gully. A pile of rubble lay beside a narrow isthmus of concrete, all that remained of the bridge. It looked narrower than the Kudu, but tire tracks in the gravel on the opposite bank suggested we could cross safely. The Puma's matte-green grill filled my rearview mirror. Johnny was too close, inviting trouble.

"Bloody fool," I muttered, "you'd better pray we're not ambushed here."

I jammed the gearshift down a gear. The bush beside the road was thick with parched trees and rough granite outcrops and rocks dotted the sandy riverbed three feet below the bridge. I pointed the Kudu down the slope at the isthmus, pressed the accelerator and hoped for the best. We surged forward, the weight of the Kudu helping to propel us downwards.

The Puma's grill receded in my mirror. Brian had put on gold-rimmed aviator sunglasses that I hadn't seen before. The oval lenses looked like small shields. Only his camouflage cap and the glasses were visible over the edge of the steel trough. The radio operator's chest and shoulders were clearly visible as the Puma tilted down the slope. Johnny's face twitched from side to side behind the Puma's thick windshield. His steel window shutters were still open.

I almost didn't hear the pings over the grind of the gears and the rattle of steel doors. At first, they seemed peaceful and far away, the sound engines sometimes made when trying to burn dirty petrol but then they increased in tempo and volume and reached a crescendo that reverberated inside the Kudu's steel shell.

"Shit," I yelled, "it's an ambush. We're being hit."

Two rockets exploded somewhere. Instinct made me duck my head. I judged that there were seven rifles firing at us. The Kudu bounced onto the isthmus and lurched to the right like an up-side-down pendulum. A soldier cursed. Automatic rifles began thundering behind me, sending cartridge casings ricocheting off the steel walls. I ground the accelerator into the floor. The Kudu lurched to the left, hesitated and then stabilized over its center of gravity. Suddenly we were off the bridge, the wheels grabbing at gravel, and then the Kudu jumped the rise at the top of the riverbank, taking us out of the killing zone. I jammed on the brakes.

"Get the fuck out," I screamed. "The Puma needs covering fire."

We sprinted toward an outcrop above the ambushers. The prickly smell of dry grass scratched my nose. I tried to flick my rifle to automatic. My thumb slipped off the safety catch. I could hear troopies on the Puma returning fire in the killing zone. Good. Brian had things under control. Our rifles sounded heavier than those of the guerillas. My rifle clicked to automatic. I glanced towards the bridge and saw the Puma crest the rise and skid onto the road's shoulder under a cloud of dust, its driver's windows still open. I started backwards to the road and the Puma.

"Radio," I yelled as soldiers fell into firing positions in the roadside ditches.

The Puma's hatch clanged open and Johnny clambered out with his rifle grasped in one hand. Rivulets of sweat streaked through the dust on his face. "It was wild," he shouted. "I was trying to get out the gully and close the bloody shutters at the same time."

"The radio operator de-bussed in the riverbed," said the bemedaled soldier.

"Get into extended line formation," I bellowed. "I want two extended lines." Panic clawed up from my belly into my throat and brain. I had never done this for real before. "We'll leapfrog through the ambush zone and get him out." Men started to move, but too slowly.

"Brian," I yelled, "where the hell are you?"

The sound of firing had stopped. Engines creaked as they cooled. The smell of petrol filled the air. A dark wet patch spread over the gravel beneath the Kudu's fuel tank as petrol trickled from a hole punched by a bullet. I told the man nearest me to plug the hole with a stick.

"We are very lucky today, Sir," he said. "They were trying to shoot the wheels."
Johnny banged the cab's hatch shut and then climbed into the bed of the Puma. A fresh magazine clicked into someone's rifle. "He's up here," called Johnny urgently. "He's been hit."

"Shit." I called back. "We'd better put a drip in him."

I ran towards the Kudu to get the first aid bag. Although I was not a medic, I had been trained to put in drips. We all had. I had volunteered to be the demonstration dummy during training and squirmed with alarm when the medic started with the veins in the top of my hand and worked upwards. This way, he had explained, if you make a bollocks of your first attempt you still have some options for our wounded soldier here. I had not put a drip into anybody since training and as I ran to the Puma, bag in hand, I prayed silently that I did it properly.

"He's dead." Johnny rubbed his eyes. "He took a bullet in the head."

Silence settled over everything—over bushes and grass, over Johnny's long shadow, over the empty Kudu, over the soldiers waiting in extended lines, over stones and rocks in the rough road, and over the killing ground in the riverbed below.

"We'll pick up the radio operator," I said, "and get Brian back to base. To the hospital." I paused for two or three seconds, considering a pursuit. "The terrs are long gone by now," I said, thinking they always hit and run, and I don't want to leave Brian here alone.

"Two inches," said Johnny. "Two inches lower and he'd be alive." He raised his hand and used his thumb and index finger to illustrate. "Two inches lower and it would have hit the steel." He leaned over and examined the steel armor. "Some bastard out there could shoot," he said. "Four or five of his rounds hit the steel just below Brian's head. Bloody brilliant grouping."

I climbed onto the Puma. On brown patches of camouflage, Brian's blood looked dark, almost black. On the camouflage's khaki background his blood looked crimson. On green patches his blood looked brown. His Adam's apple was shaved clean, but there was a bullet hole through the patch of unshaven beard on his cheek. I reached down with my fingers spread and pulled his eyelids closed. His eyeballs bulged under my fingertips. Blood spread around my boots.

Scattered near Brian were a handful of coins. I began picking them up one at a time, I don't know why. They may not have even been his. Some were recently minted ten-cent pieces. Others were shillings from Rhodesia's days as a colony. The brightest was a copper penny. A meniscus of blood clung to the edges of the largest coin, an old two-shilling-and-sixpence piece that reminded me of the coin Father Armstrong had paid me in Sunday school.

We left Brian on his back where he'd fallen. Johnny crossed his arms over his chest and covered his head with a combat jacket. We drove slowly to avoid jolting him too much on the rough road, to show our respect. His blood had started to dry by the time we got him to hospital. Someone called a chaplain. I went home to my hut.

Even before I opened the door, I smelled formaldehyde. I shoved the door open with my foot. The stench scraped my nose. With a howl, the camp's tabby bolted from the shack, brushing between my boots. I hurled a curse after the cat and wished that Brian had kicked it the day before. The formaldehyde had started to dry from high spots on the rough concrete of the floor, but a trail of paw prints led from the bottle to the door. The fetus lay on its side among shards of glass. The jar's shiny tin cap rested near its head. A sliver of glass rested across its legs.

I left the fetus there and began walking around the camp, forcing myself not to think. I split a Baobab pod into two and savored the cream-of-tartar seeds inside. As their tart flavor spread around my mouth, guilt seeped into my head. Brian's death had nothing to do with luck or with unsettled spirits. I kept walking. Someone brought me a Shumba, but it tasted vile, so I poured it out and watched the dry earth swallow the amber liquid. The grizzled old soldier with six medals approached me, saluted and said he was very sorry about Brian, that I needed a way to honor him, a good man. I nodded. It was a good idea. There had been no real need for Brian on the Puma, and he would be alive if I had not ordered him to join the escort. I shook my head, as if chastising myself for the way I had treated him. Like all of us, he had really only wanted a little friendship and recognition. But now he was dead and there was nothing I could do about it. I kept walking, trying to remember the good in him. I recalled his excitement at rescuing the fetus from the ruined clinic, a fetus that was now lying on the floor of my quarters in a bed of glass shards. That I could do something about. I about-faced and strode to the kitchen, where a portly cook, after some cajoling, gave me a large-mouthed bottle and a beaker of clear vinegar. I placed the fetus gently into the bottle and covered it with vinegar.

We buried Brian three days later. I was one of four pallbearers. His casket, a simple mahogany one, bruised the muscles of my neck and shoulder while, opposite me, Johnny squirmed as the wood cut into his shoulder. The casket smelled of fresh varnish but a small scratch near my head marred its finish. The wreath atop it smelled of lilies, roses and fresh cut stems. The priest, a man I'd met earlier, stood at the head of the grave, wearing flowing robes of green and purple that reached to the ground. Soldiers and civilians stood near the grave. We came to a halt and silently lowered the casket. I glanced up at the priest. He nodded and handed me a small wooden casket.

This casket was pine stained with linseed oil. I knelt on the fresh dirt beside the grave and felt stones pressing into my knee. The morning sun was still low, and the grave was filled with shadow. Silently I mouthed the chorus to a hymn I had sung as a child: All things bright and beautiful, all creatures great and small, The Lord God made them, the Lord God made them all.

Then I reached towards Brian's casket, careful not
to fall, inhaling the smell of the fresh, moist earth. As my
eyes adjusted to the gloom, the blackness in the grave
dispersed and color crept into the flowers on the casket.
Roots and twigs crept from the earth walls. Clods of green
grass appeared in one corner and scars left by a spade
took shape. I dropped the small casket the final few inches
and heard it land on Brian's casket with a soft thud. For a
long moment I gazed at the two caskets, feeling drained
but at peace with the world, and then I slowly rose to my
feet, closing my eyes to shut out the blinding light.

## About Lionel de Maine

*Something Moved* was a long time in the making. A work of fiction, the story is set in the very real turmoil of the 1965-1979 chimurenga or bush war in what is now Zimbabwe but was still Rhodesia when I left in 1978. Almost everyone was embroiled in the conflict in one way or another. One day, someone showed me a fetus preserved in a bottle that he had found in a destroyed mission hospital. While collecting war souvenirs is nothing new, taking a preserved fetus as a souvenir was certainly unusual and worthy of a short story.

I wrote the first draft over 25 years ago with the goal of including it in a collection of stories about growing up in Africa. Life intervened and I never completed the project, although two of the stories, *Leopard Skin* and *Floppies* were published. I had forgotten about *Something Moved* until, looking for a piece to contribute to this collection, I stumbled across it on my computer.

The bones of the story changed little over time, but as the characters deepened I tried to surface the interplay of luck, spiritual beliefs and religious beliefs. By the end of the story they form a triangle that is not quite resolved, I hope, leaving open the question of whether the narrator really believed that luck or unsettled spirits had no role in Brian's death. In his death, reality touches fiction: the exactness of the two-inch margin that Johnny emphasizes to highlight Brian's bad luck reflects the experience of a draftee I knew. Ambushed on his first day, a bullet meant for him struck the armor plating exactly two inches–he measured it–below his head. Was it luck?

# For The Love of a Dog
## (John Rosskopf)

I woke up early at my girlfriend's house on Saturday morning. I didn't wake her. I let her sleep in. I quietly put on my khaki shorts and a gray, pocketed T-shirt with the sleeves cut off and headed out to her pool. It was already eighty degrees this early August morning, and the weather reports were for between 108 and 112. For the ninth consecutive day with no relief in sight! Sometimes it gets hot in Sacramento. It hasn't really been cold in winter for several years.

Climate change. The only other place on earth I'd been where temperatures could get so uncomfortable so quickly was Iraq during the 2000's, when my Explosive Ordinance Disposal team had been attached to a 7th Calvary Battalion in a forward operating base near Baghdad.

Today, I walked out of Aisha's bedroom slider and sat on the edge of the pool. I dangled my feet in the warm water, and even though the water was warm, it still provided relief. The sun hadn't risen enough yet to bear straight on me. There is a bank of eucalyptus trees on the east side of the backyard. They have a sweet smell I like. They also provide sunblock of sorts. I took in a deep breath, leaned back, and enjoyed the best part of the day. There would be no work today, and Chastity, Aisha and l would simply enjoy ourselves.

Chastity is Aisha's nineteen-year-old ward, and lives here while she's studying to be a nurse. Aisha, of course, is my girlfriend. She's a doctor at Kaiser Downtown Commons, not far from my office on the first floor of the Wong Center near 5th and J Streets. My office door says, "Jake Powers and Associates, Private

Investigation." The "Associates" is just there because I think it sounds good. But really, it's just my administrative assistant, Pablo Carrillo, and me.

I was by myself for an hour until Chastity came out wearing a skimpy two-piece bathing suit. Chastity is alabaster white with blond hair. Aisha insists she put on sunscreen when she's outside half naked. I had trained myself not to look when she was dressed this way. After all, I

was more than old enough to be her father.

"Hey Chastity."

"Hey yourself."

"How ya doin'?"

"Fine, and you?"

"Fine too."

Our conversations in the mornings usually began this way.

She sat next to me to my left and dangled her feet in the water, too. She had been a runaway at fourteen and was trafficked for two years up and down I-5 and I-80. Then she had started a call girl business with a few friends who had ditched their pimps, and all were saving money to get out of the business. Aisha had found her and taken charge when she heard of her background. When the other ladies left the business, Chastity took up Aisha's gracious offer.

Chastity was the daughter Aisha had always wanted. Chastity treated Aisha like a mother she never had.

In another hour Aisha opened the slider and announced breakfast was ready. Chastity and I got up and dried off our legs. We walked through Aisha's bedroom and then to the kitchen for some eggs, toast, vegetarian sausage, and coffee. All three of us were trying to lay off meat. Fish was okay, but who eats fish for breakfast?

We sat around Aisha's butcher block kitchen table, once I had set the table for the three of us, and Chastity had procured filtered water for us from Aisha's dispenser on her stainless-steel refrigerator.

Aisha is the love of my life. She is a little shorter than me (I'm just shy of six feet) and has beautiful caramel skin that she keeps soft as the cotton balls she uses at work. She has her black hair in box braids that hang down to her shoulders. Her eyes are gentle and as green as the most expensive jade. Her face is soft and intelligent. Her teeth are perfect, except her two bottom front teeth push slightly into each other. A small defect too small to warrant braces. But her smile is bright, and she uses it to get what she wants from me. She's quite successful. She poured for all of us the deep, dark, rich Ethiopian coffee she gets at a coffee house on Broadway. You'd think coffee this dark and rich would be bitter but it's not. It's my favorite.

"What are you guys going to do today?" Aisha asked neither of us specifically.

"I'm just going to kick back," I replied, "after I go home and feed Ernie."

"I need to study for a test Monday in Algebra II, so I'll have to get to that once I enjoy the outdoors until it's too hot to stand," Chastity replied.

Ernie is my black and white former tom cat who adopted me, with my permission. He is an indoor/outdoor cat, and he'd spent last night outdoors. His right ear has a nick in it from his former life fighting over female cats. When he sprayed once in my house, a trip to the vet put an end to all of that.

Aisha and I live only a couple of miles apart. She has a beautiful ranch style home on American River Drive down the street from Rio Americano High School. I live in Woodside on Howe Avenue and Sierra Boulevard. Aisha had inherited her house as the spoils of a divorce, and my wife had gotten our house in Roseville. So I had to find alternative digs, and I had at the Woodside condos that had been converted from apartments.

Aisha served us. We could have gotten the food ourselves, but this is a part of homelife she enjoys. Sometimes Chastity and I help in the kitchen, but usually it's the province of Aisha. She'd remodeled the kitchen and had it just right.

"I'm going to sit around too. Maybe I'll do some reading, but I'm not going out in this heat. That's why we have air conditioners," Aisha said.

After we ate breakfast, Chastity and I put the dishes in the dishwasher and cleaned up the table. That's one part of kitchen life Aisha doesn't mind that we've taken over. She's into the cooking. The clean-up is the responsibility of the diners.

I put on my Sperry's and drove home to feed Ernie. He was waiting for me when I pulled into my covered parking spot at Woodside. He mewled and did figure eights through my legs as the two of us walked to my front door.

"How you doing, pal?"

He got audibly louder. Ernie's a smart cat. Sometimes I think he actually understands what I'm saying. Quite frequently we have conversations. But usually, it's just me who does the talking while he stares at me as I rub his head and neck. I fixed his kibble and wet food and refreshed his water. He has a water dish at the front door too. I refreshened that also. He ate like he hadn't eaten all night. He hadn't. Then I putzed around the house for a couple of hours and let Ernie out and drove back to Aisha's. I parked in front of the house and let myself in. When I got there, there were two people anxiously waiting.

Aisha was sitting on one of two soft, white stuffed side chairs, and a woman and a boy were sitting on the matching white couch. The two women were chatting amicably. I had never before seen the lady or the boy, and didn't know them, but Aisha introduced me to Mrs. Regina Morales and her son Diego. We all shook hands.

Regina was an attractive, honey-colored woman of about thirty-five, with black hair and obsidian-colored eyes. I noticed her immaculate red nails. Diego was the typical kid. I'd guess eight years old. He had on a colorful T-shirt and jeans with black tennis shoes. He had hair the color of his mother's but his was tussled. After exchanging pleasantries, I excused myself, and got up to go back to the pool area when Aisha said, "Jake, where are you going?"

I looked back in ignorance of the situation, and said, "out back by the pool."

Then Aisha said, "JA-AA-KE. Regina and Diego have come to see you."

I stopped in my tracks. I was surprised to hear that, but I got the not-so-subtle hint from Aisha I was to stay and sat back down. I looked at them and said to the mother and boy, "What can I help you with?"

Then the story began. Mrs. Morales spoke first.

"My little Diego, bless his heart. He has this little dog named Lucky. Nothing much. Just a mutt. But he loves this dog very much." Miguel started squirming in his chair. "He walks the dog down the American River Parkway every morning before it gets hot. About a week ago, he's walking his dog, and he takes it off the leash. But not just the leash. He undoes the whole collar. The collar contained all the contact information...the dog's name...who owns him...you get the picture. They're walking on the dirt trails among the brush and the trees. Then a deer runs out and Lucky chases him. Diego goes running after his dog, but it continued following the deer and didn't come back. We haven't seen him since. The boy is heartbroken.

"We know Dr. Moore from around the neighborhood. We heard she has a friend who is a private investigator. I think that's you. We thought you might be able to help. Anything I'm forgetting Diego?"

Diego put his head in the cushion, like he was hiding. Then, I could hear him say quietly, "No." I was embarrassed for the boy.

"What have you done to find Lucky?" I asked.

"We've done everything. We passed out flyers. We walked the neighborhood. We put a reward in the neighborhood news. We've been following social media. But nothing."

"And what do you think I can do that you haven't?"

"Don't be negative, Jake," Aisha said. "Mrs. Morales has read about you in the newspaper and knows you know your business."

"Yes, but..."

"No buts. How can we find Diego's dog?"

I could tell Aisha was taking up Mrs. Morales cause, and she expected her big time PI boyfriend to help. How could I say no?

"Do you have a picture of the dog?" I asked.

"Oh yes." And Mrs. Morales got out a color picture and handed it to me. It was of a small black and white dog who appeared to be in a backyard. It looked like a terrier mix. Its left ear was bent over, like it was permanently bent in half.

"Is this ear always this way?" I asked.

"Yes. That's the way we got him from Mr. Bradley. He found him," Mrs. Morales said. "Do you think you can find him again? We can pay."

"Well, it sounds like you've done everything I would."

"Jake," Aisha said. I could see I wasn't getting out of this.

"But I could give it a try. I don't know if I'll have any more success than you've had. But I'll do my best. Does Diego have a dollar?"

"Yes. He has a bank with a number of dollars."

"If he gives me one of his dollars, I'll be on retainer for the weekend, and I'll look for the dog."

"Diego will be happy to give you a dollar. Right Diego?"

I looked at Diego, and he was squirming again on the couch. He'd look at me then he'd hide his face back in the puffy white cushion. In one of the times he was looking at me, he managed to utter, "Yes."

"Okay, it's done then. Jake Powers and Associates will dedicate the weekend to finding Lucky. I don't know if we'll be any more successful than you were, but we'll give it a try."

Aisha and Mrs. Morales smiled and looked at Diego, who was still squirming.

Aisha said, "I told you he'd help."

Like I'd had a choice.

"First, I'll need to ask a few questions."

"Okay," Mrs. Morales said. "Shoot away." She told Diego to listen up because he might have to answer one or two. She straightened him up, but he still looked away, only now at the floor.

"Can I have the picture?"

"Yes, of course."

"When was the last time you saw the dog, and where were you?"

"Diego, do you want to answer these questions?" Mrs. Morales asked.

Diego just buried his head further into a cushion.

"We live down the street on Regency Circle. It borders the American River Parkway. We have a gate in our fence that gives us direct access. Diego went out the fence and walked east...how far would you say you got Diego?"

Diego just squirmed and hid his face in the cushion again. The kid was taking shyness to a new level.

"Anyway, it was somewhere east on the Parkway. It wouldn't have been too far. I don't let him walk far away from the house. But there are always nice people on the Parkway. We don't have any homeless or others I might be afraid of this far from the Sacramento River. He and his friends from the neighborhood play out there a lot. That would have been a week ago yesterday that Lucky got away."

"Is the dog chipped?"

"What do you mean, 'chipped'?" Mrs. Morales asked.

"You know. The vet puts a little computer chip in at the neck. Then if someone finds the dog, the vet or the SPCA can find the ownership information."

"He's not chipped. We never did that."

"I'll see what I can do. But remember, no promises. If someone else has the dog, we might have to involve a lawyer to get it back."

"I'll do anything to get Lucky back."

"Okay then."

"Oh, thank you," Mrs. Morales blurted. "Diego, you should say thanks too."

Diego looked up from the cushion and said a quiet, "Thanks."

I told them it was nice to have met them, and I'd be back in touch. Aisha showed them outside and the ladies' conversation continued out front on the porch. I got up and took the picture with me and went out back to the pool again. Chastity was sitting in the shallow end of the pool, up to her neck. I sat in a lawn chair. I'd have to develop a game plan, and it would take Chastity, Pablo, and me, if we were to have any chance of finding the dog over the weekend.

"Chastity. Can you take a little time away from your studies today?"

"I don't know. What do you need?"

"I'm going to ask Pablo to make up some flyers with a picture of Diego Morales' dog and contact information. Then I need you and Pablo to walk the streets of the neighborhood,
especially the streets that border the Parkway, and pass out the flyers."

"Is that what that was all about in the living room?"

"Yep."

"How long would it take?"

"Only a few hours. Let's say from two to five this afternoon. I'll walk the Parkway doing the same thing and looking for the dog. Then the three of us will meet back here and see if we've had any luck."

"Is Pablo alright with this?" she asked.

"I think he'll be, but I'll have to call him and ask."

"Okay, if he's in, I'm in."

"Thank you. This means a lot to Aisha. She expects us to come through, but I think we're good with just the effort."

I got Pablo on the phone and told him what was going on. Since he had no plans, he was all in too. I met him at the office, and he made up some flyers. He's a whiz with the computer. The photo of the dog looked perfect, and the information looked professionally done. We made two hundred copies and then drove back to Aisha's.

I told Aisha what my plans were, and she thought it sounded great. She said she'd make dinner for the four of us, and since Pablo lived alone, I figured he'd like a home-cooked meal. When I told him about it, he said, "Of course."

So, Pablo, Chastity and I set out at 2 pm, each with a mission to accomplish. We all wore light clothing and hats to withstand the heat, which was now well over 100. We all put on copious amounts of sunscreen. Chastity and Pablo had looked at a map and had divided up the neighborhood. I figured I'd walk the Parkway as far as I could in an hour and a half and then walk back. I would pass out flyers and look for any sign of the dog, although the latter effort probably wouldn't bear fruit. Someone had taken the dog for their own or it had met its fate. I didn't want to think about it, but mountain lions sometime come down from the foothills and into the Parkway chasing deer. It doesn't happen often, but as man encroaches upon nature, the inevitable clashes occur.

I walked east down the Parkway after entering it at the high school. It was Saturday and those people daring enough to brave the Sacramento August heat walked and rode bicycles. But mostly, the trails were empty, the walkers, joggers and bike riders having had their fill earlier before the temperature got unbearable. But I had made a promise to Aisha and the Morales family and I'd keep it. I got as far as Ancil Hoffman Park and I turned around without having any luck. When I got back to Aisha's, Pablo and Chastity were back and they hadn't had any luck either. Both looked wilted and whipped. I'd walk farther than Ancil Hoffman Sunday morning before it got hot. Maybe I'd have more luck then.

"We got rid of all the flyers, but no one had seen the dog," Pablo said.

"Everyone was sympathetic, but no luck, pardon the pun," Chastity added. She smiled.

Chastity showered and got ready for dinner. I guessed she'd study afterward. I hoped I hadn't ruined her exam. Pablo went home too, and said he'd be back. Since he only lived off Fulton Avenue in the Timberlake Condominiums, he didn't have far to go. I peeled off my clothing and jumped into the shower in Aisha's bedroom. I keep some clothes at Aisha's house, so I put on some khakis, a polo shirt and boat shoes.

We ate at 7 pm. Chastity and I set the rosewood table in Aisha's formal dining room. Shortly after Pablo got there, we all feasted on salmon, baby yellow potatoes, and green beans. Of course, before this, we all had a salad. Aisha insists on having salad with every dinner and Chastity and I had become used to it.

After dinner, Pablo bid adieu, and Chastity and I cleaned up. Then Chastity excused herself and said she had to study. Aisha and I sat and read in the living room for a couple of hours, with Aisha sipping on a good strong red. I had a Tanqueray over. I was reading a biography of Ernest Hemingway and Aisha was studying the most recent medical journals. We went to bed at about 11 pm and fooled around a bit before we lay back and started talking about the dog.

"Do you think you have any chance of finding him?" Aisha asked.

"This is what I think. The dog has been gone for over a week. I doubt if it could live by itself on the Parkway. I mean, what would it eat? There aren't many trash cans and I've never seen strays along the paths. All the dogs I've seen are on leashes. What's more likely is that someone took the dog home and adopted it. You know. Gave it a name, bought a fancy dog food and water bowls, and now it's part of their family. What else could have happened?"

"You make it sound pretty bleak."

"We have to be honest. I know the boy wants this dog back, but I doubt if that's going to happen. On the other hand, there are dozens of little dogs at the SPCA that would love to be adopted. Maybe the best outcome here is to get Diego a new dog."

"I don't think he'll go for that as long as there's a smatter of hope Lucky can be found or will wander back. What are you going to tell Mrs. Morales?"

"I'll tell her just what I told you. The young man has to get over it. There's disappointment in every young life. If he wants to maintain hope for a little longer, fine. But I tried my best today. Chastity and Pablo walked countless streets. The dog's gone. Diego has to face it."

"I guess you're right, but I was hoping for a better outcome."

"Tomorrow I'll go down to Ancil Hoffman Park and look around. There's a lot of acreage there a dog could wander around in, and maybe a better chance of finding food and water. But if I can't find him then, it's over."

With that, we both rolled over and tried to get some sleep. I was tired. I'd probably put in ten miles today, which is a lot when the weather is so hot. I was sure Chastity and Pablo would sleep well too, although when Aisha and I came to bed, the light was on in Chastity's room. I could see it under the door. I guessed she was still studying. First thing I'd do tomorrow was go back to Woodside and feed Ernie. Then I'd go back to Aisha's and eat breakfast, and then go to Ancil to look for a dog I was sure would never be found.

Ancil Hoffman Park is a green oasis in a vast expanse of urban sprawl. Located in Carmichael just to

the southeast of Fair Oaks Boulevard, it contains a famous wildlife area, a
popular 18-hole golf course, equestrian trails, hiking trails, several picnic and sports areas, and is populated by various species of the original oak trees and other tall shade trees that have been planted to provide relief from the sun. The American River Parkway runs through it, as does the American River on its southwestern border. Riprap has recently been placed in the river for salmon and steelhead spawning, and various species of wildlife call the park home, including deer, racoons, opossums, skunks, and a variety of bird species. It is a birders' paradise. It covers almost 400 acres.

I had walked from Rio Americano High School just to the edge of the park yesterday, but that was enough for one day. I had passed out flyers and talked to people all to no avail. Maybe today I'd be luckier. I parked in the picnic area and began walking trails near the nature center. A red-tailed hawk soared on the thermals above. A woodpecker whaled on a nearby tree in a rapid fire yet rhythmic beat. It was just after noon and the sky was deep blue in color and the blazing sun was almost at its zenith. I had on shorts and a long-sleeved collared polo shirt, and I wore a straw hat for protection against the sun. For those areas that were still left exposed, I had applied sunscreen, liberally. Rivulets of sweat still dripped down the small of my back.

I didn't expect to find Lucky running free. But if someone had "found" him, maybe they would be out today walking him on a leash. As anticipated, I had no luck in the nature area, and no luck when I walked the area of the bike trail I had not gotten to yesterday. That left the picnic area where dogs were permitted on a leash, provided you cleaned up after them. I walked the picnic area and saw many pure and mixed breeds of dogs, but no Lucky. There were some small black and white mixed breeds, but they were dissimilar in a variety of ways. When I got to the end, I noticed a black and white dog with a bent ear that piqued my attention. As I got closer, I gained more and more hope. The dog was on a leash held by a little girl of about 12 with pigtails, red hair, and a freckled face.

I didn't want to scare her, so I watched from a distance in a discreet manner so I wouldn't be identified by someone as a pervert. After half an hour, she and the dog sat down with a family in the shade of a canopy of tall trees on a large blanket. Warily, I approached. There were two older boys playing frisbee and a man and a woman who were sitting drinking soft drinks. I walked up to the gentleman and struck up a conversation. I wasn't chatty and would soon get to my point. But I couldn't just walk into their picnic area and accuse them of having someone else's dog. I'll have to admit it. I was anxious.

"Nice day today, isn't it?" I said to the slightly overweight gentleman, who had his shirt open and a belly hanging out.

He warily answered my question in the affirmative, and stared at me, probably wondering what I wanted.

"You ain't one of those Jehovah's are you?" he said. "Because we're Catholic."

"No," I answered. And I got out a folded-up flyer out of my back pocket and handed it to him. "I've been looking for this dog since yesterday, for a little boy who lost it a week ago. It looks an awful lot like your girl's dog, doesn't it."

"That's Spotty," he said. "We've had him since he was a pup. But about three years ago, he got out of our backyard as dogs do, and ran off. My daughter was sick at the time. Then three days ago we were walking on the Parkway, and we found him again. I have no idea where he'd been, but someone had obviously been giving him food and water. He was healthy. It's kind of a miracle, I guess."

"How can you be sure he's the same dog, because he looks an awful lot like the dog I'm looking for?"

"When we got him as a pup, we got him from the SPCA out on Florin-Perkins Road, and they neuter and chip the dogs they put up for adoption. We took him to Dr. Jones at Manzanita Veterinary Hospital when we found him just to be sure, and she read his chip. Sure enough, Spotty had come home. My daughter is happy as can be. She wouldn't take another dog when I offered after we'd lost him, she just wanted him back."

He got a business card out of his pocket and handed it to me as he introduced himself. He was Mr. James Cooper, salesman, American River Pools. I got out my business card and shared it too. He read it and said, "Sorry it's not your dog."

I thanked him for his time. I walked back to my car and drove back to Aisha's. I didn't know how I'd break the news to Diego, but perhaps another dog from the shelter would satisfy him. There was only one way to find out. When I got back, I told Chastity and Aisha what I'd discovered. They were sorry for Diego but happy for the little girl who'd found her dog after three years. Aisha called Mrs. Morales and told her the bad news. Aisha said we had the father's contact information if she wanted to contact him. Aisha suggested we all go to the SPCA and see if we could get another dog. Mrs. Morales said she'd call back after talking to Diego.

After a late lunch, Mrs. Morales called back. Aisha handed me her cell. Mrs. Morales said Diego understood, and he'd like another dog if he couldn't have Lucky back. He'd cried for a little while, but then got over it. She said she would give Diego a week, then take him to the SPCA

Adoption Center if he still wanted another dog. The center was closed today, anyway.

"Mr. Powers, Diego and I can't thank you enough for your efforts. We can pay, like I said."

"It's alright Mrs. Morales. It was a pleasure to help. I have to admit, it was a million to one it would end this way. The chances of finding that dog after a week were minuscule."

We clicked off.

I poured a double Tanqueray over with three olives and Aisha poured a glass of red wine.

Chastity didn't drink alcohol, so she brought an orange juice out to Aisha's living room where we all sat down and chatted. The weekend had been productive, just not in the way Diego and his mother had hoped. At least now they knew how Mr. Bradley had come to have the dog, and that it was back with its rightful owner. I knew Diego wouldn't be happy for some time. But a new dog would go a long way toward assuaging his unpleasant feelings.

"See," Aisha said. "Mrs. Morales was right the whole time."

"How could she have known it would end this way?" I asked.

"That's not what I meant. I meant she and Diego knew if they hired a big-time private investigator, the mystery would be solved."

"Oh, now you're just teasing me."

The three of us laughed.

## About John Rosskopf

John Rosskopf is a Sacramento writer, lecturer, and attorney. He is also an avid and voracious reader of murder mysteries, and a few of his favorite authors are Michael Connelly, Robert Crais, and Joe Ide. Now Mr. Rosskopf is introducing his own private investigator series, as he follows the adventures of his fictional private detective, Jake Powers. After his latest book, *Requiem for Tuesday*, Jake is transitioning to a Special Agent for the California Department of Justice.

When asked why this story, Mr. Rosskopf said, "Two of my principal characters are Jake Powers, butt-kicking PI, and his girlfriend, Dr. Aisha Moore. Often Jake is involved in violence and Aisha is patching him up. I thought for this story it might be good to use the same characters, but take the violence out of the scene. Why a missing dog? That's a great question, and perhaps asks for an explanation of the creative process. My wife is always reading the neighborhood news on the Internet and often she tells me about a missing animal. Perhaps that entered into my subconscious and played a part in creating the subject matter. It just felt good to do something different."

Mr. Rosskopf lives in Sacramento with his wife Marian, and his two cats, Max and Tiny. To learn more about John Rosskopf and the Jake Powers Mystery Series, please visit John's website at johnrosskopf.com.

# Korea Tales
### (Retold by Marcia Ehinger)

My father was a medic in Korea during the late 1940s. Within a week of the new commanding officer's (CO) arrival at the 38th Parallel, Dad had been scheduled to face a
court-martial.

This new CO had decided the American soldiers' life was too lax. That might have been true. My father's usual summer garb was a baseball cap, a white t-shirt, fatigue pants and a pair of sandals made by the locals.

The CO ordered all vehicles to be locked up in the motor pool garage at night to keep them safe. My father objected.

"Sir, the aide station ambulance needs to be available at all hours and should remain parked outside." The CO threatened him with court-martial.

A few nights later, a lone soldier was on guard at the fuel dump nearby. It was very cold as he made his rounds. At some point, he got the brilliant idea to take the metal cup from his mess kit up to the nozzle of a kerosene tank. He poured a bit into the cup and lit it on fire to warm his thinly gloved hands.

"What could possibly go wrong?" you ask. With hands stiff from cold, the guard didn't quite close the tap and dropped his cup while setting it aflame. The badly burned soldier was rushed all the way to the hospital in Seoul using the ambulance that had been waiting outside.

On the following Monday, my father stood outside of the aide station, cleanly shaved and wearing his dress uniform. *I'll never see my sergeant's stripes again. Wonder where I'll end up in the brig?*

Nobody showed up to drive him to his court-martial. No further mention was made of locking up the ambulance at night.

******

My father was a teenager in the early 1940s during World War II. He had to get a draft deferment to finish high school because he turned 18 years old prior to graduation. One third of his neighbors and classmates were of Japanese heritage. Those teens are quite evident in his junior high yearbooks, but are gone later, as their families were forced into relocation camps.

After three years of fighting in the Pacific, moving from island to island to dislodge the Japanese forces, the U.S. military was preparing to storm the beaches of Japan. My father received extra weeks of survivalist training for that eventuality. Then, he studied to be a medic. During that time, the atomic bombs were dropped on Hiroshima and Nagasaki (August 6 and 9, 1945, respectively), essentially ending the war.

Korea was free from Japanese domination and Soviet troops moved in. A decision was made among the Allies that Moscow would be in charge north of the 38th parallel and Washington, DC, would be in charge south of the border, officially splitting the country.

Dad was redeployed to the new demilitarized zone between North and South Korea. On the troop ship sailing across the Pacific, my father was one of the few who was not seasick and not bored enough to spend endless hours pounding silver dollars into rings on the deck rails of the ship. He went below and volunteered to be a baker. It didn't take long for the crew in the officers' mess to realize that he could barely boil water. He was handed a broom and a mop but allowed to swap cleaning duties for samples of fresh-baked breads, and leftovers of dessert pastries.

In Korea, my father was assigned to man an aide station on the 38th parallel. There weren't many Americans stationed there, so he spent most of his time dealing with refugees and the local villagers. Many people were fleeing from uncertainty, a Chinese civil war, and Soviet troops in the north. At the aid station, people could stop and rest; women went into labor and birthed their babies. Dad immunized refugees. He joked about saving the local headman's grandson from "terminal impetigo" (a nasty Strep skin rash) by bathing him in an oil drum with warm water and strong soap, then applying an antibiotic cream. The headman thanked him with a pair of brass chopsticks. For other kindnesses, he began to receive fresh eggs and vegetables, left anonymously on his doorstep early in the morning – precious gifts from local farmers who had little to spare.

One sunny day, Dad was free for lunch and made his way down the hill to the base mess tent for a hot meal. As he was sitting down with his tray, a couple of hefty bearded Soviet soldiers in heavy wool coats entered the tent. Each was armed with a Kalashnikov rifle.

*Oh crap*, thought Dad. *Those Soviets are so careless with their weapons, and they never clean the damn things. Bet they're ready to fire.*

As if to prove that safety was not their concern, the Soviets started waving their weapons as they made grand gestures to punctuate their conversation. They seemed quite happy to be there for lunch. Maybe they'd already had their vodka ration for the day.

They couldn't speak a word of English, but chattered jovially as they walked over to an empty spot. One man laid his gun on top of the table. The other set his upright at the end of the table, barrel up. They loaded their trays with food and returned to eat.

Everyone's eyes were on them when the genial hubbub went from full volume to zero. The Kalashnikov standing at the end of the table began scraping against the wooden supports on its way to the floor. All the soldiers figured it was loaded and knew there was no safety catch on the automatic weapon. They all held their breath as Dad wondered, *What'll the damage be when that thing hits the ground? Who's gonna die?*

Thunk!

Thankfully, one problem with not cleaning and oiling a gun regularly is that it may jam rather than fire.

The whole room inhaled at once.

The unperturbed Soviets kept on talking and eating. They finished their lunch and left, waving their Kalashnikovs to say good-bye.

******

Other aid station stories included those about soldiers who would drink anything that might contain alcohol, including shoe polish. For a while, a rumor circulated that you could purify such products by pouring them through a loaf of white bread, which made the cooks crazy when they couldn't figure out where all of the bread was going.

One drunk man arrived for care freaked out because he pee'd green urine after stealing and drinking the medicine cabinet's rubbing alcohol which had been dyed blue to discourage soldiers from taking it.

After much imbibing one night, there was a Western gunfight in the barracks with real pistols and live ammunition.

And, what do you do after a hot, bumpy Jeep ride
and you don't want to lose any of your beer when it spews
from the can, you don't have a punch can opener, but you
do have
a bayonet on your rifle...?

## About Marcia Ehinger

Marcia Ehinger was born in Los Angeles, California, and started life in her grandparents' citrus orchard near several tourist destinations. She spent time diving, delivering mail, and translating bathroom signs into Spanish and Miskito in Nicaragua before graduating from the University of California, Santa Cruz. (Go, Banana Slugs!) Then, she attended medical school at the county hospital which inspired the "Code Black" television show, which portrayed a critically overcrowded and understaffed emergency room.

Marcia writes in various genres, both poetry and prose, and realized too late she wanted details from some fascinating characters in her own family. One grandmother was an outgoing snazzy dresser in the Roaring Twenties who partied with Hollywood starlets and small-time gangsters.

Her mother's stepfather started work in the oilfields as a teenager. Despite his lack of formal education, he self-published a book of poems, some of which related harrowing experiences in World War I. Her mother descended from generations of men who had volunteered to serve in the American military since colonial times. Having no brothers, she joined the Women's Army Corps in World War II and led a unit decoding secret messages at the Pentagon. Proudly wearing her uniform on a trip to New York City, she was spat upon by bums in the Bowery who proclaimed "only whores and lesbians" would join the Army. Marcia's father's stories are included here.

Since retiring from medical practice, Marcia has had more time for writing. Anthologies have showcased her poetry, speculative and historical fiction. She creates monthly nonfiction articles for the online magazine,

California Update. A dystopian novel and a series of children's books featuring California wildlife are in the works. Her website is under construction and will soon house a blog dedicated to amazing individuals who "died too young." [marzoo.net and subsidiary sites, coming soon]

# Back Home On The Edge
### (Gregg Matson)

The Old Man was on the wagon again. Bob Sutton could tell, because there was no booze anywhere in the house. He knew the Old Man's hiding places. This was not a pleasant discovery, for a couple of reasons. One, this had been going on for about five years now, with the Old Man sobering up after each particularly awful bender. And while the Old Man didn't go crazy like he did when he was drinking, he was always mean when he was dry. Two, Bob Sutton had a hangover and wanted a drink.

Not a good time to come back home.

He had no choice, though.

The landlady had been there at the door, first thing in the morning—silent, everything having already been said. The thirty-day eviction deadline would be enforced.

Scheffler and Boyd had already moved to new digs, and they weren't inviting their old pal and roommate, Sutton, to move in with them this time.

A month ago, there was the certified letter, which Ken Boyd had signed, informing them about their legal obligation to leave the apartment. Simple, legal, unavoidable. The three had sat around sullenly when Boyd finished reading the letter.

Phil Scheffler broke the silence. "Your fault, you know, Bob."

"Mine?"

"You and your stupid friends Friday night."

Sutton blurted, "It's Boyd's fault."

Boyd turned to Sutton. "What the hell are you talking about?"

"You didn't have to sign that receipt when that postal jerk delivered the letter."

"Oh, Christ."

Sutton continued. "Not only that, you should have talked to the landlady Friday night when she asked to see you."

Boyd shook his head.  "Why the hell should I talk to her? If it wasn't for you and your loudmouth friends, she wouldn't even have been there."

"But she wanted to talk to you."

"That's because my name's on the lease. But you were the one who needed to shut up."

Scheffler looked at Sutton. "Then when you picked up Richards, down the hall, and threatened to slam him against the wall—"

"I never did that."

"He had witnesses, said you did."

"Ahh, that's bullshit. Richards is a goddam jerk, but I never threatened him like that."

Boyd said, "Friday night was different."

"Bullshit."

Scheffler waved his hand downward. "We've been through this a hundred times in the last five days. Richards bitched about the noise, and you and your friends knocked on his door. You grabbed him by the shirt—and now we're out."

"I didn't do that!  I'd remember!"

Boyd said, "What did your friends say you did?"

Sutton threw up his hands. "Haven't talked to them."

"Well, anyway," Boyd said, "now we've got to move." He stomped into his room.

Scheffler yelled, "Goddammit, I hate to move!" He went to the refrigerator and got a beer.

"You bastards did your share of carousing too," Sutton groused.

Shaking his head, Boyd said, "Oh shit."

As he packed his things to move back home, Sutton needed but two trips to the car. Then he drove back to his childhood home. He went to his old room and put everything away. He'd gotten rid of his old college stuff...there wasn't much. In two years he'd barely passed thirteen units—none of them this year.

Vietnam was calling.

He had volunteered for the draft, just to move things along.

Maybe the Old Man would like that, knowing his son was at last growing up, taking responsibility. Well, the Old Man wouldn't like it—he didn't actually like anything—but he might be a little less hostile, knowing Bobbie wouldn't be back home for long. And there was that patriotic thing. The Old Man had been in WWII.

Of course, he also knew that the Old Man could be less hostile, less unreasonable, than he usually was—yet still be intolerable. He flopped on his bed and tried to sleep away the hangover.

Late in the winter afternoon, Mom came home from work first. Through the slit under the bedroom door, Sutton saw a light go on. "Bob?" Mom called.

"Yeah, Mom, come in."

Mom opened the door and turned on the bedroom light. "How are things going?" she asked, in a tone that really demanded to know what the hell he was doing here.

"Fine. I'll be back home for a while. Until I get the draft notice."

Mom's face turned hard, shrewd, as she pondered the next move. He'd seen that face a million times in his twenty years. "How long will that be?"

"Hard to say. I signed up last month. Shouldn't take too long."

"Well....What happened with your apartment?" She knew he didn't want to come back home any more than she or the Old Man wanted him to come back home.

"Didn't want to pay rent for the full month. I could be drafted any day."

"You still have your job?"

"Oh, yeah. In fact, I've put in for extra hours this week."

"That should help. I'd better get dinner started."

Realizing he wasn't going to sleep, he threw on his jacket and went out to the garage. He started to work around Mom's car, tidying up the place. There wasn't much to do. The Old Man was a fanatic about neatness when he was sober. Anything out of place, anything soiled, anything untrimmed or unswept, was a tragedy in need of an instant scorched-earth remedy. Still, it might help if he wasn't lying down when the Old Man came home.

In the fog a car stopped. A door opened. Little Brother got out, waved at the people inside the car as they drove away. Little Brother, getting bigger all the time, glanced at Bob's car, parked along the sidewalk. Shaking his head and smiling grimly, he walked up the driveway, into the garage. "Hey."

"Howdy. How was basketball?"

"Not bad. Does the Old Man—"

"Not yet. He's not drinking?"

"Nope. Two weeks."

"How is he?"

"Not too bad. Nervous."

"The usual."

"Yep. Well...I'd better get to my homework." Little Brother went inside.

Sutton continued his useless puttering for about fifteen minutes, until the car rolled into the driveway. The Old Man's head turned to look at the car along the sidewalk. The engine turned off, but no one got out of the car.

Bob Sutton's head had cleared in the cold air, but now he felt nauseous again. He waited, trying to appear calm, for the car door to open. He could see the Old Man's form, peering out through the foggy dusk. He knew the Old Man was wishing he didn't see what he did see in the garage.

Finally, the door clicked and opened. The Old Man stepped out, walked up the driveway, into the garage. "Hello, Son."

"Hi, Pop."

"What're you doing?

"Oh, just checking out the garage.  Seeing what needs tidying up."

The Old Man smiled mirthlessly. "I can see you're doing that. What I want to know is what brings you here."

"I'm going into the Army. Hoping to stay here until I get the notice. Should be any day now."

"You still have your job?"

"Sure do."

Father looked at Son, their eyes communicating briefly, trying to overcome twenty years of miscues. Then the Old Man set his face to a quirky, strange, yet familiar expression. "Tell Mom to keep dinner warm. I'll be right back." He turned around, got into his car, and started the engine.

# Boys
## (Gregg Matson)

The year—Chandler thought it was 1968—didn't matter. Never mind the month or day. Suddenly everything was moving too fast for minor details. The guys had been patriotically passing around a joint.  Then the shooting had started, and Chandler thought it might still be going on, but that wasn't important.

The pain was gone. Yep, all gone.

He was back to sunny days, playing Army in the suburbs. "Got you, Chandler!"

"No, Doyle, you missed!" The debate could go on, interrupting the game. They could almost get into a real fight over a play fight. But it was fun. And the next day, the boys would be back playing Army, no matter what...unless they were playing baseball, or football, or just riding bikes in search of adventure. Those were sunny days and good times.

There were war movies on TV, in black-and-white, all the time: *A Walk in the Sun*; *Bataan*; *Fighting Seabees*; *12 O'Clock High*; *Sahara*. All the time. And there was a neighborhood full of daddies, who had actually lived through all that.

Doyle had been the first to join, first to come back on leave. Nineteen, with a skinhead—serious, ramrod-straight...and he knew the lingo. "Real tight, you bastard!"

"Get squared away, puke!" "Rack." "Geedunk." "Nam." "You will be on time!"
Doyle knew what he was talking about, all right. He had warned him, "Don't join up, Chandler. You'd never make it."

But another year down the line, Chandler realized what had been obvious all along—that he hadn't been making it on the outside either. Jobs, girls, decent grades—all hard to come by, and getting tougher all the time. So, Chandler had joined up, for the same reasons Doyle did.

But Doyle had been right. Chandler wasn't going to make it.

And that wasn't important, either.

## About Gregg Matson

Being a "baby boomer" I came of age in the fifties and sixties. Growing up took longer. I entered manhood during the Vietnam War era, and was fortunate to have never been in the military service. I say this not as a matter of either shame or pride, it just happened that way. I believe I served my country to the best of my ability by staying out of the service. I have terrible problems with authority figures, which the military frowns upon. I would have honestly tried to do as I was told, just to avoid trouble, but I believe I would have rebelled at just the wrong times. I could not have been of any use to America from a federal prison cell.

My stories are about general life of young men during that time. They are based loosely on the experiences of some of my friends who did enter the military.

I have tried to honestly record the thoughts, feelings, and deeds of members of my peer group. I hope to convey at least a hint of the general confusion that pervaded the country in those times.

My literary success has been quite limited, but nonetheless, words will not leave me alone. I have published two books: *Living in 1984—America's Flirtation with Fascism*, and a detective story called *Healthy, Wealthy, and Dead*. I write a blog for *The Daily Kos*.

As the result of several day jobs, I live the comfortable life of an old hippy, and I still try to keep an eye on developments in the world at large. I am amazed to witness the similarity of current events to those of my younger days.

# The Living Nightmare
### (P.L. Clark)

I am a surgeon in Napoleon's army, a highly skilled man with the tender hands of a healer, covered in mud and soaked to the skin from the constant rain. Would I ever be dry and warm again?

The road is a rutted swamp with mud that stinks of horse manure and unnamed filth. Each step was a sucking battle as the soft, deep muck tried to steal the boots from off my feet. Waves of cavalry and infantry had torn up the road, and cannon caissons had finished destroying it as they traveled to the next battlefield.

The ambulance and medical wagon wheels are sunk halfway to the hubs in the slimy mud. Wounded or not, every man who could help aided the horses as they struggled to move the vehicles forward. Minute by minute, I labored against that cursed wheel. Were we making progress? I couldn't tell.

My muscles bunched and burned, and I feared every step would be my last as I pushed with all my strength to move the wagon one centimeter at a time.

Today's battle raged ahead of us. Cannons roared their might in thundering voices. Boom, boom, boom across the field, with the crackling volleys of infantry fire making a sharp counterpoint as the two sides of this eternal conflict fought to kill each other.

Would this war never end? I yearned to be back in my private practice, away from the madness of senseless death, but here I was, as stuck as the wagon I fought to move.

Aside from the ambulances, we had three wagons. One had medical supplies, tents, and general provisions, and the others held the wounded and dying from earlier battles who we hadn't left in the care of civilians.

Minute by minute, hour by hour, I labored against that cursed wheel. Indeed, such struggles were an unending hell for all the terrible sins I must have committed, even though I could not think of a sin worthy of this torturous work.

At midday, a man dressed in a French cavalry dark green uniform rode toward us. "Get off the road," he said, pointing to a clearing. "Set up the tents."

We surged ahead, with the promise of stopping, struggling to move the wagons off the road. It was time to prepare ourselves for receiving the horrible results of the onslaught. I dreaded the agony I would inflict on already suffering men while trying to help them survive.

The continuous roar of cannons and rattle of rifle fire was the backdrop against getting the medical tents set up.

Silence fell, and the ambulances left the camp to bring in the injured. A steady stream of the walking wounded, many supporting others, followed them as they returned.

What seemed seconds later, the ambulance wagons arrived, creating chaos with triage and shouting as we sorted out those needing immediate help and those who could wait.

Time passes, as it does in the rush of trying to do too much with no time to think beyond the moment.

I've spent long hours saving the ones I could and hating it when I had to turn away from the ones, I had no way to save.

The smell of mud, blood, and bodily fluids from the numerous surgeries clogged my senses, and I found it hard to breathe as I cut and stitched, resolved to do my best to save them. The screams and moans of the wounded waiting their turn at my table made it difficult to remain sane amongst the results of the madness of Kings and Generals, greedy for power and glory.

When I finished treating the final man, I staggered out of the tent and almost stumbled onto the pile of shattered limbs and body parts I'd removed from the wounded to save their lives. The knowledge that two-thirds of them would die today or tomorrow from infection and gangrene crushed my soul. I have no way to save them all. Dear God, no way.

A young boy of seven or eight approached with a cloth and a basin of water so I could wash the blood from my hands and face.

I thank him as my aide de camp arrives with a flask, and I take a deep draught of the fiery brandy. With the potent drink surging through my body, I relaxed and pulled out my pipe, creating a cloud of smoke to take away the smell that coats my mouth. Too soon, I hear the wagons coming again, accompanied by the wails of the wounded.

I returned to my surgery and got back to work. When the fighting stops for the day, the stretcher-bearers and ambulances scour the site, looking for the living among the dead. The battle had been horrific, and the brave men with grievous wounds waited for their turn on my table with stoic patience.

At last, my surgery stays empty, and it is time to do my rounds to see how many men my bloody day's work has saved for a while. Perhaps they'll live to see home again.

God knows, I don't.

The groans and moans of the wounded join the smell of blood and gangrene, vomit, and the foul stench of bowels evacuating upon the death of those souls who had given their ultimate for their country.

Two women and a young boy work among the cots and pallets. The younger woman carries a basin of water to wash a patient. She waves at her son and sends him on a mission, and he scurries away. The older woman holds a young soldier in her arms as he cries for his mother. She holds him long after he dies before she beckons an orderly over to take him away.

My hands and shoulders ache, and I am exhausted as I walk among the cots and pallets of the wounded. So many young men died, but many will live while missing a body part.

How will they survive? Will France become a nation of cripples forever seeking alms? Will my country survive this madness? Will either side of this war feel it was worth the pain and death it caused?

My aide de camp enters my tent and hands me a cup of mulled wine. "It's late, and you must rest. Tomorrow will come early."

"Thank you," I say and sip my wine as he picks up the soiled clothes I'd dropped, tsks at me, and leaves.

I try to relax, but my thoughts won't settle. When I sleep this night, the faces of the war's veterans missing a limb will haunt my dreams as they have every night. Some curse me, but others smile and nod, glad they're alive.

Yes. Tomorrow will come soon, and I'll try to save as many men as I can until this war ends. When that time comes, will I ever have a night's sleep free from the nightmare I'm living?

# About P.L. Clark

"The Living Nightmare" is a story about a day in the life of a surgeon in the Napoleonic army.

In 1967, I had one of three recurring dreams each night: pushing the wagon, after surgery, and at the end of the day. These dreams continued for two weeks and have remained as clear and vivid as the nights I dreamed them even sixty-seven years later. I believe in reincarnation, and because dreams usually fade in time, and this one has not, I know this is a picture from another life lived before this one.

\#

Penelope Clark, known as Penny, writes under the pen name P. L. Clark. She is a creative writer who dabbles in multiple genres. Her books are available on Amazon.com: P.L. Clark author page.

Always a voracious reader, in 2010, while driving from Everett, Washington, to Elk Grove, California, a song on the radio sparked an idea that became a trilogy, which became the basis of a five-book series, Dangerous Gifts.

Since then, she has written and published over eighteen books and has more characters shouting in her mind, wanting their stories told, too.

She is a retired accountant, a widow, and a co-founder of the Elk Grove Writers Guild. An introverted hermit, she enjoys reading, writing, gardening, and watching the wild turkeys, and an occasional peacock strutting past her window each evening.

# The 75th
(Mark Paxson)

When he was a boy, they called him Tad. Thaddeus Adams. Somewhere along the way, he was a cousin of those Adamses. The ones who signed the Declaration of Independence and served as President and assumed other positions of power and influence. In the family tree, Tad was far too removed from those Adamses to have anything to do with such things.

As a child, Tad spent his free time playing in the creeks of Ohio, where his family had a farm. In the summers, he splashed through the creeks in bare feet, yelling like he thought an Indian might. He had a stick he imagined was a gun until he was nine and Papa gave him an old musket that no longer worked. It made no difference to Tad. That useless weapon slayed many an Indian in the summers, their blood-curdling battle cries cut short as he fired bullet after bullet into the gathering hordes.

In the winters, Tad didn't go as far afield in the cold and snow. Instead, he bundled up and sat on an old log that rested along the edge of the creek that rippled through their farm. The quiet of the snow-blanketed ground and the crisp cold air entranced him as he sat and watched the creek babble along until the deepest dark of the winter froze it over.

Tad was mostly by himself when he roamed the wilds of the Ohio countryside. His mother died before he reached his first birthday, so there were no more Adamses along his branch of the family tree. There were other boys he befriended at school, but they rarely played together outside of the schoolyard. Farms were too far apart, there was always too much work to be done. Papa too tired. For the most part, when he wasn't in school or doing chores assigned to him by Papa, and at times it seemed there were always chores to be done, Tad spent his days alone.

Until the night, when they sat down for dinner, with a fire in the hearth. Most nights, they rarely spoke. But every now and then, Papa would tell the boy stories of the other Adamses. The men who had helped build the country. When he did so, Tad listened raptly, not wanting to break the spell that seemed to be cast out as the words spilled from his father's lips.

Those nights were almost as good as his days spent chasing down Indians and watching the creek in the coldness of winter.

One such night, as Papa wound down and began to pick up their plates, Tad asked him, "How come you never did any of that stuff?"

For a moment, Tad thought he had angered his father with his question. The look on his face in the flickering candlelight was like the one Tad saw when he failed to do a chore or talked back. But it passed this time and his father sat back down. "Not all men are made for such things. I was never good with books and schooling. I had other things on my mind, I guess."

"What other things?"

"Well," Papa paused for a moment, staring into the fire, "I was a bit of a hellion back then. Couldn't sit still." He laughed oh so briefly. "Kind of like you, I liked to roam and run a lot more than I liked maths and readin'."

Before Tad could say more, his father reached out to tousle his son's hair and stood up to take the plates away. "Besides, farming fits me. I don't have to make speeches or convince anybody of anything. Other than to get the cows to share their milk and the chickens to lay their eggs. I don't know how I could possibly manage to do what Uncle John did. It scares me just thinking about it."

"Scares you?" Tad had never heard his father say such a thing, had never seen any sign of fright in him.

"Ayeah. There are things that scare me, son."

That night as he closed his eyes, Tad told himself that he would be like those other Adamses. He wanted to be famous. To be known for something.

For Tad though the path to being known wasn't clear. Much like his father, he preferred the outdoors to the indoors. He preferred trees to books. And so, he continued to roam the land and barely paid attention at school.

One summer afternoon as Tad splashed through the creek, he suddenly came to a halt. Before him was something he had never seen in all the years he had claimed the creek as his own. Or a somebody.

On a rock at the edge of the creek sat a young girl. By Tad's estimation, she looked no older than eight or nine. Her long blond hair shimmered in the sunlight as she leaned over to splash water on her feet and shins. As she did so, without looking at Tad, the girl spoke to him, "You make a lot of noise, don't you? Do you never stop to enjoy the silence broken only by birds and rushing water on rocks?"

"Wh-wh-where did you come from?"

The girl continued to splash water on her feet and still did not turn to Tad. "Where I come from doesn't matter. What matters is you."

Tad looked around to see if there was anybody else near. Somebody who might be connected to this girl he had never seen before. There was nobody.

"You wish to do great things. Am I right?" With that question, the girl turned to him and smiled.

"How ... How do you know that?"

"Am I wrong?" She shrugged. "It is something most boys of a certain age wish."

Tad shrugged without answering directly.

"No. I'm not." The girl paused and put her finger to her chin. "I don't remember the last time I was wrong."

"You're just --"

"Thaddeus Adams. You will have an opportunity to achieve great things. Very soon, there will be a great war. The nation's fabric will tear. Brother will fight brother. Many lives will be lost. This will be your chance to prove yourself and to rise above your surroundings."

Before Tad could respond, the girl began to fade and soon she was gone, leaving the boy wondering if she had ever actually been there. He looked around before slowly making his way home. *A great war*, he thought to himself. *When would it happen?* He was fourteen years old. *Not old enough to figh*t, he thought. *But in a few years. Maybe.*

Tad hoped the war would not come and go before he had a chance to prove himself. No matter how odd it was that the girl herself had come and gone, Tad found himself believing her. She had given him a hint to how he could achieve greatness. In a war. It gave life to all of the fantasies he had acted out while battling make-believe Indians in the creeks and lands around him.

Tad was not a boy who paid much attention to the world around him. He didn't need to know much to splash in his creek and slide by in school. He knew nothing of the impending storm that was coming to America.

That night, he asked Papa if a war was coming.

"It sure seems like it. If Lincoln is elected, it looks like we may just go to war."

"Why?"

His dad paused before answering. It was the first time his son had ever asked him such a question. He had become accustomed to his son's seeming lack of interest in the world. In fact, it comforted him and gave him assurance that his son was like him. Just wanting to farm and be left alone by the world.

"It's about slavery. The South depends on it. Lincoln appears to be opposed to it. Although nobody seems to be exactly sure about that." He closed the book he had been reading. "It's just a lot of people not talking to each other is what it is."

"Will that lead to war?" Tad began to clear the table without his father asking, an unusual event.

"Why do you ask?" his father asked, peering at him from behind his bushy eyebrows.

"I dunno," Tad said with a shrug. "Do you think I'll be able to fight if there is a war?"

His father's glance grew a bit darker. "Is that what you want? To fight in a war? You would leave the farm to … what … find glory in battle?"

"Yes. I wish to be a soldier. To fight for something." Tad dumped the plates in a tub that he then put on top of the stove, allowing the fire underneath to heat the water for a moment or two before he scrubbed them clean. "Surely ending slavery is something to fight for?"

While he worked, Papa watched him. His son's stated dream saddened him for he thought that Tad would always want to remain on the farm. Maybe marry one day and build his own home on the land, eventually taking it over once he got too old to manage things. He hadn't realized that Tad was like so many other boys of his age, believing that war was about glory.

"Son, come. Sit down."

Tad did as directed.

"You should realize that war is an ugly, ugly thing. If there is a war between the North and the South, it will be brutal. Many will die. If you were to go and fight and, even if you were to come back alive, you will be a changed man. You'll see things and lose something. You'll never be the same." He reached out to touch Tad's cheek, caressing it lightly before removing his hand. "War is no way to achieve glory for most who fight in such things."

A few months later, Lincoln was elected and the rumored possibility of a war became a deadly reality.

States throughout the North began to enlist volunteers to send to the war. Battles raged from the shores of the Potomac River in the East to the banks of the Mississippi in the West. Ohio was no different, forming many regiments of soldiers, who were drilled and outfitted and then marched many miles from battle to battle. Many of them to their death. Many more returning home with grievous wounds, not all visible.

Tad was not in the first group of soldiers to serve, but as the war dragged on and the casualties mounted, it eventually came for him as well. The United States Army, desperate for men, ignored that he was not yet eighteen.

Tad's Papa objected, but his words fell on deaf ears.

"Papa," Tad pleaded, "this is something I need to do."

"You're too young. Just too young."

"If others are going to fight, then I must as well. Isn't the Union something worth fighting for? Shouldn't we sacrifice as so many others are for such a noble cause?"

"I can't lose you."

For the first time in his life, Tad saw tears form in his father's eyes. That moisture slowed him down. But only for a moment or two. For Tad, this was his time. To prove himself. To become a man. "I'll be back."

"You can't know that."

Tad had nothing left to say as they stared across each other at the dinner table, and in the morning, he left without a word while his father was working one of the fields.

It was 1862 when Tad left home, joining the newly formed 75th Ohio Infantry Regiment. Soon he was off to war. Fighting in South Mountain, Chancellorsville, and eventually Gettysburg.

It wasn't long before Tad realized that his father had been right. War was a brutal, horrible thing to experience.

Tad's first real experience of war was at Boonsboro Gap. Until that bloody battle, Tad's experience had mostly been marching from here to there, and back again. Only to march to a different there and then back again, while the generals of the North dithered and stalled.

After days of marching through Maryland in pursuit of Robert E. Lee's army, the battle was drawn along the mountains of Maryland, across three gaps. Lee took up positions and the Army of the Potomac sought to use their superior numbers to deal a crushing blow to the South's favored son.

As the Union soldiers marched into Maryland, Tad's regiment, exhausted from days of marching and fueled almost entirely by coffee served hot that morning, formed up aiming at the Boonsboro Gap. Tad tried to block out all around him and stay alive. He succeeded in the latter, but not the former. The sounds of bullets hitting flesh filled the air. All around him, men fell screaming. The man to Tad's left was shot in the face. He thought he might never forget the sound of the bullet hitting the man's teeth, producing a sound like a clay pot falling to the ground and shattering. The man, who had fought for the North from the beginning, fell to the ground. In his final seconds, he grunted and screamed through his shattered face before quieting.

Officers gave orders, only to fall before the final words were past their lips. New leaders stepped into the breach and gave different orders.

"Charge!" A bullet zinged through the man's chest and he fell in a heap, his eyes lifeless.

"Hold!" said the next. His horse was shot out from under him and as horse and rider fell, the man broke his neck.

"Move!" said the third. And so they did.

The 75th Regiment fought on, pushing the Rebels back. All around him, men who had survived kept loading and firing. The Rebels were running. Not forward but back.

In the midst of it, Tad felt separated from himself. As though he was watching from above. This man who was firing his rifle and advancing. Bullets zinging past. Other men falling. Puffs of smoke arising from the rifles shimmering in the heat of the day.  That man was him.

Victory seemed near until new orders went down the line. "Fall back."

It was Tad's first experience with what the more grizzled veterans had told him as they marched towards Boonsboro. The battle of Boonsboro Gap was a Union win that the generals and commanders of the Army of the Potomac were too cautious to pursue to a complete victory.

Here they were, successfully attacking the heart of the Rebel line, pushing them back, and instead of pressing their advantage, they were expected to retreat?

All Tad could do, as many of the men around him were doing, was shake his head and mutter as he fell back. Orders were orders after all. As he did so, Tad came back into his body. Breathing heavily. Sweating heavier. Hoping he could get to safety now that the Rebels were at his back.

Once he got back to the regiment's camp, where they were relatively safe from any Rebel counterattacks, Tad found a spot to rest. There he discovered a bullet hole in one of his sleeves and a fraying of his cap that suggested bullets might have paid  visits there as well.

Tad wondered, not for the first time, about the wisdom of his mission. He could still picture the girl in his head and hear her words. Was he a fool for having believed in her? Was he a bigger fool for believing that he would rise to prominence because of this war? How could being one of thousands fighting for the cause, fighting to stay alive, help him achieve the fame he sought? These were the thoughts he went to sleep with that night.

The months that followed saw Tad's regiment doing more marching to and fro, but little fighting beyond a skirmish here and there. Soon enough, however, Tad once again marched into battle, this time in the Wilderness and Chancellorsville. He proudly marched with nothing more than his gun and rucksack slung over his shoulder as his regiment crossed the Roanoke and approached the Wilderness, an overgrown tangle of vegetation that surrounded the area.

Once again, after days of exhausting marching and fueled by coffee and hardtack, as Rebel soldiers yelled their fierce battle cry, a chill spread throughout Tad's body. He and the rest of the men began to fire and several of the enemy dropped, but still more came. Soon, the man to his left fell with a bullet through his neck. The Rebels kept screaming and approaching. Relentlessly, it seemed to Tad.

Other men along the regiment's line were falling as a voice entered Tad's head.

"You must fall back. The Rebels will soon take this spot and any who remain will be killed or taken prisoner. Fall back."

It was the voice of the young girl. Although it had been several years since that moment on the creek, he knew it immediately.

"But ...," Tad finished loading his rifle and put it to his shoulder and fired off another shot. He thought he saw a soldier fall barely 20 feet in front of him. He felt nothing at the idea of having killed or wounded another man. He was the enemy after all. "... we were told to defend this position to the final man if necessary. I have not received orders to retreat."

"If you wish for greatness, this is not the place for it." Tad could hear the sigh in her voice. "Look around you."

Tad did and saw that many of his comrades were falling back and that he, in fact, was the most forward soldier in his regiment. With Rebels quickly approaching.

He turned and ran and as he did, he felt the sting of a bullet in his arm. Tad cursed, but didn't stop. He ran with everything he had.

The wound was minor, requiring nothing more than a simple bandage. But once again, Tad found himself idled as the generals of the North and South moved their men around like chess pieces on a giant board.

Soon enough, however, Tad and his regiment of Ohio volunteers were on the march, along with tens of thousands of Union soldiers and many more Rebels. In the humid heat of summer, they marched miles each day until, like a magnet, they were drawn to the small town of Gettysburg.

On July 1, they arrived with a new commander, Colonel Andrew Harris, who led them in a street-by-street battle through the town before taking a position on East Cemetery Hill. They spent a day digging trenches and trying to fortify their position as well as possible, knowing with virtual certainty an attack was coming.

At dusk on July 2, the Louisiana Tigers, a particularly fierce band of soldiers in Lee's army, attacked the 75<sup>th</sup>'s position on the slope. Cannons fired, splashing deadly projectiles into the midst of the men from Ohio.

Tad found himself ducking and praying more than he had in the earlier battles. There seemed to be a ferociousness to the assault that had been absent before. Even with the rebel yells and charging soldiers firing away. There was something different about this battle, something that caused Tad to wonder if his end was near.

Men fell on both sides and still they came. The Union troops on the hill held their ground and kept the Rebels at bay. Tad did his best, firing as he could. He was able to drop several men in Rebel gray. Some close enough he could see the looks on their faces as they were hit – shock, surprise, pain, loss – and fell to the ground. Their screams could be heard over the roar of the battle. Even their quiet murmurings as their final moments approached floated above the noise and reached Tad.

The chaos of war enveloped him that night and the next morning when the Rebels renewed their assault. All Tad knew was a feeling of exhaustion and that he could do nothing more than keep loading and firing. Loading and firing. While wondering where the girl was now.

He had come to think of her as his guardian angel, sent by some unknown force to protect him and guide him to a life of meaning once the war was over. Now, with death all around and more coming, she had abandoned him in his hour of greatest need.

As he thought this, he rose to shoot at an approaching man in gray rags. The man was barefoot and looked like he had not eaten in days, but he had a gun in his hand and he was pointing it directly at Tad. In the same instant, they fired their guns. Tad felt the bullet rip through his gut as he saw the other man fall.

As the other man did, so too Tad fell to the ground. A slow-motion drop turned him around and left him lying on his back, staring up at the clear blue sky. Tad felt nothing in that moment. Just wonder at the sky and a calm sense that he was about to die and that it was okay.

"Oh no," came the voice.

Tad turned his head and saw the girl approach him. She walked slowly through the wreckage of the battlefield and seemed unaffected by the bullets and more that continued to shred both sides of the line. The girl eventually reached him and sat on her haunches.

Tad opened his mouth to speak but no words would come.

"Sssshhh," she said, placing her finger on his lips. "You don't need to say anything."

The girl used her sleeve to wipe his face of the sweat and grime that covered it, as well as the tears that were beginning to leak from his eyes. As he lay there with his guardian angel over him, the sounds of the battle faded. Tad no longer felt the fear that had enveloped him for the past two days. He was at peace, but there was one thing he needed to know.

"I'm sorry, Tad," she whispered. "It was not supposed to end this way for you."

He coughed and opened his mouth, croaking out the words, "What is your name?"

She continued to wipe at his face before answering. "They call me Cael."

"Cael," he repeated as he closed his eyes and drew his last breath.

******

From the monument to the 75th found at Gettysburg today:

*Arriving at Gettysburg from Emmitsburg July 1, 1863, the 25th and 75th Ohio Infantry advanced beyond the town and, under a heavy cannonade, took position here, supporting Battery G, 4th U.S. Artillery. During July 2 and 3, they held an advanced line on East Cemetery Hill, and early July 4 led the advance into the town.*

## About Mark Paxson

Generally, I come up with a vague idea and then I see if I can turn it into the story. I originally was going to write about a Vietnam veteran who was tormented by his dreams. Dreams of what the lives of his fallen comrades might have been like had they lived. It didn't seem like much of a "story" though, so I decided to switch gears and write about a soldier in the Civil War.

I've done a lot of reading about Lincoln and the Civil War in recent years and wanted to see if I could capture it. But ... I also wanted to include an element that was a bit fantastical and that is where Cael came in. Back in the early part of the 19th century, there was a lot of "religious awakening" going on in America, so I felt a character like Cael wouldn't be completely bizarre.

And that is how *The 75th* came to be. I think I could have done a lot more about the brutality of that particular war, but the story is what it is.

I've been independently publishing my fiction for about a dozen years. Two novels, two novellas, and two short-story collections later, I'm still writing. Although it goes much slower now than it did when I first started writing about 20 years ago. You can find my books on just about every on-line book retailer. Just search my name.

I also blog about politics on Substack (Blog title: A Dead Horse), have a couple of other blogs, including Writers Supporting Writers. I am into photography, want to learn to paint, and to figure out how to get back into a more regular rhythm of writing.

# Gray Matter
### (Fred Nolan)

"This line here. You see where it comes in?"

"Maybe."

"By comes in, I mean it comes into your life. It could be an injury, or a loss of some kind. Somewhere around age fifty-five."

"Fifty-five?"

"I take it that age means something to you."

"It might. What year would that be, 2023?"

He and your mother kept a Christmas tree up twelve months a year. If only for that, you were sure he would see another December. After all, falling was no longer a concern: he mostly slept; he passed his days in a wheelchair. For the last several months he had been too weak to roll out of bed. To push himself off the mattress would have taken more arm strength than he had. More core strength.

If you could take back one thing, though, it would be showing him that marked-up photograph in early 2022, the day he went to the hospital.

Mom had called a few hours earlier, and sent a text. You missed both. Your wife came home, rushing upstairs: "Check your phone, I just talked to your mom. There's something going on with your dad."

"Something how?"

"She said he's acting weird he was doing something with his pants."

"With his pants?"

The answer was so unexpected you took comfort in it. And your mother confirmed it: "He was taking so long in the bathroom I went and checked on him. He couldn't stand up. He couldn't work out his pants."

"Work them out how?"

"He couldn't figure them out. It was all I could do to get him in clean clothes."

You found him at the hospital, not in a bed, not attended, but alone in the waiting room. He was upright in a wheelchair with a surgical mask pushed low, under the chin.

His expression, christ. Hopeless and irate. His face changed when he recognized you, but it didn't change all the way.

"Fred, hi." His voice was weak. No volume to speak of. You weren't sure if you were only lip-reading.

"Dad! Are you alright?"

He was hard of hearing but kept cotton in his ears anyway, because of chronic ear infections. Mom was afraid he would start losing his consonants, then entire words. "From there you lose everything," she said. "Your mind is too focused on sorting through vowels to focus on anything else."

She insisted that, at his age, hearing loss was a direct cause of dementia. His world would be pure sensory feed. Pure nonsense.

"Dad?"

He kept in that unhappy trance and you sat in an adjacent seat, trying to coax him out of it. You told him about the kids, your job, old friends, the pandemic. You showed him pictures from your phone, swiping right over and again.

Who knows, maybe putting him through a slow-motion epileptic light show was to blame.

But you'll never get past the idea that it was the modified snapshot of the sedan.

"Look at this one, see what we did to Buddy's car? You can paint over any photograph with just your finger. So we repainted the entire thing like this, like this, like this. See?"

You kept waiting for him to chime in, but he stayed quiet.

"Just one brush stroke at a time. We did it with a picture of the dog, too. Look. See?"

His expression was shifting between impressed, unsettled and heartbroken. He handed you his water, thanked you, then a tear spilled down his cheek as he bit down hard, leaning far back and away, a horrible cord of blood and saliva working its way toward his lap.

You shouted for help in no specific direction, with no one person in mind.

"It's a seizure. He's seizing."

That was a man directly behind you. Not hospital staff. A bystander with an elderly mother.

Now a middle-aged woman joined him. Both were caring for retirement-aged patients, that much was clear.

"Thank you."

You already had a hand on the unknown man's shoulder, leaning on him and listing like a boat.

It wasn't until January when you asked what your wife meant by gray matter, which she mentioned all the time. It had been years now, and you always figured she was talking about the intellect, or the brain itself. But it was something to do with your daughter's theater competitions, too.

In that case, then, did it refer to an actor's talent for putting herself into character, or into the logic of the play? We only have eight minutes to get the gray matter in place.

She did not mean smarts, though. She meant the physical props, the unit set, as state rules call it. In formal competition, every school gets the same building blocks, a fixed stock of three dozen plywood constructions, built to stand in as doors and windows. Walls. Built in ramp shapes, or platform and pillar shapes.

They were drab. Canvas-colored. Conspicuous only in how lackluster and pervasive they were.

Think of them, if it helps, as structures built out of green screen. With stage lighting, a few cheap decorations and context clues, the audience sees almost anything.

Perhaps, then, the phrase circles back to the mind after all. Our gray matter tells stories with their gray matter. Our sense of reason turns creative, we tell ourselves stories with these dull, ashen surfaces.

Better said: our mind itself becomes theater.


Dad was a born storyteller. A born writer, too, though he rarely wrote. In prose his voice was similar to yours, no surprise. But there were plenty of differences, too. His style was rhythmic. Inquisitive. Tap water pure.

He read more than he let on, until he discovered *One Hundred Years of Solitude*, which he recommended to everyone. He kept your mother updated chapter-by-chapter, often page-by-page. He would play tricks by inventing scenes, and sewing them into the fabric García Márquez had written. He would give her a choice of three plot developments, and have her guess which one was his.

But they were all his.

In one example, Remedios becomes sure that messages are written to her in the town's rubbish. She spends hours waist-deep in the trash pit, looking at food scraps, her hands and arms cut repeatedly on rusting tins. In another, Jose comes upon a nest of sickly, fledgling birds, which he is convinced are the souls of his family members, though he cannot find his bird anywhere.

In a third, the people of Macondo observe storm clouds forming higher and higher. In time the accumulations are sun-high, and the characters are scalded during rainfall.

After your Madagascar trip—for which you took quinine, then suffered hallucinations—he reminded you he took the same treatment for a year straight, in Vietnam. You and he talked about co-authoring a novel, set in a war the soldiers fought in their heads. In this telling, quinine-drunk, malaria-drunk infantry would shoot nonexistent targets with blanks. It shocked you how receptive he was to the idea.

Who knows, maybe he inwardly wanted it to be true.


The first you heard about sundown syndrome was 2017. The old man was already showing signs: forgetting people, forgetting events. His temper was a minefield you had to walk across. Once he forgot he had a new car and called your mother from the garage, in a panic about it, the odd vehicle there, in place of his.

But this sundowning—would it be so bad to relive his childhood streets? If he had to suffer dementia already, would there not be some benefit to going back to the old-world department stores of his youth, what with the indoor-circus atmosphere and world-expo architecture? The ice cream shops and burger joints? The mid-century stovetops, the chickens in every pot?


"Did you kill anyone?"
That was a question for a child to ask. Yet the way he avoided it, you were still asking during your teenage years. Even as college graduates, your friends asked:
"Did you see much action?"
"Action?"
"I guess I mean, did you shoot anyone?"

"I don't know. I got shot at. I shot back. I just don't know."

You and he had the conversation so many times it was a record with a skip. He was saying that all the time now: "I don't know, I don't know," almost no matter what the question was.

How are you dad? I don't know, ask your mom.

Are you ready for lunch, dad? I don't know.

During the worst of it you started calling your wife, sobbing before she picked up the phone. You were past hysterical, saying things like, "He used to make combat jumps, he founded companies and traveled the world. Yet now the staff has him playing games like Name Five Kinds of Plants and Which of These Shapes are Round."

It was becoming rare to see him engage with others. Rare, but necessary. We all need to see each other through someone else's eyes, if only on occasion. You'll never forget his hip surgery, for example, when he briefly spoke to the Kenyan nurse in Swahili.

It was one of your daughter's shows the last time it happened, at least in any meaningful way. Two of the elementary school cast members saw his Vietnam hat and pulled him aside, thanking him for his service. He handed each of them an honor coin. They were moved; both had difficulty accepting it, but it was clear, both of them wanted to.

That night you said, discreetly, to your wife, "Thank god for theater kids."

She never asked what you meant. She didn't need to. And she replied at once:

"Every one of them."

Youth theater exhausted him. That is where you most noticed his decline and his hearing loss, exactly as your mother had said. He would lean over and tell her—

quite loudly, though he believed he was whispering—that he had missed a joke, missed a line. Or that he simply did not know what he was watching anymore. The gray matter onstage turning grayer.

After the seizures and covid diagnosis, he spent three nights in the hospital. The staff handed you a clear plastic bag with his pants, socks, sunglasses, and a few other personal effects.

At the bottom of the bag was his Vietnam hat and a few honor coins.

You didn't realize until later: It was all I could do to get him in clean clothes.

Mom sent him to the emergency room—and to your daughter's play—ready to see him engage again. Ready to see him through someone else's eyes.

In the months before the rehab facility, he kept asking about the family in the front bedroom, the one who locked the door; the one with the dog. He asked about a car he thought was pulling into the driveway. He asked what parties they were going to throw.

"Who all is coming tonight?"

"Honey, it's just Fred and Amber and the kids."

"The kids?"

He would ask to go to the office, or go snow skiing. At first mom was unsure about playing along. Her answers were literal, too blunt, though in time she let him pretend: "You know something? I think Breckenridge has skiing. It's far, though. I'll pack tonight and we'll leave in the morning."

He asked repeatedly to speak to his mother, who died when he was thirty-eight. He asked to go home, as he put it, even if they were in the living room of the house, in the place they'd owned for more than thirty years.

Once he asked her, "What's your phone number?"

She told him, and checked to make sure he had keyed it in right.

"And what's mom's phone number?'

'The same one."

"So if I wanted to call her, I just—?" He pantomimed pressing the green digital button at the middle-bottom of the screen.

"That's the one."

He did, and her phone rang at once. She left the room, telling him she was going to let the dogs out. When she was out of earshot she said, into the phone, "Hi Johnny!"

You cannot imagine how she pulled this off, it only matters that she would try.

"Mom?"

"It's me. How was your day?"

"I don't know. Some of it was good. Some of it was bad."

"Why bad?"

"I don't know, but it's best not to dwell on it, right?"

The house must have been full of digital echoes. All part of that wonderful green screen, or perhaps gray screen, in the long year between his covid seizures and the nursing home.

"That's right. That's so right."

"It's good to talk to you."

"It's great to talk to you, honey, but I have to go. I love you, thank you for calling."

"I love you too, Mom."

She hung up, and returned to the kitchen, where he was hanging up, too.

"She had to go."

Your mother's birthday is Veteran's Day. And November eleventh marked three weeks that he was gone.

The moment had been slow to come, after a gradual decline over the course of hours. You couldn't help the idea the hospice nurse was making it up to be rid of you, to take the room back, to send a final bill to Medicare and be done with it.

Your grandmother was fifty-five when she died, and her name was June. Your favorite names have always been month names.

Dad would shout for hours in those last months, after the staff woke him, or cleaned him, or adjusted him in his chair. You heard him from the elevator, where you had to key in a passcode to get in or out.

You were sure he would celebrate one more Christmas, though. And in his sundowning, in the stories he told himself, he seems to have. The last time you saw him awake was late September, and he was shout-singing *Adeste Fideles* in Latin. He was in unbearable pain but beneath the suffering was a thing you didn't expect. An odd contentment, maybe. Distant, but it was there.

But Venite adoremus, in passable Latin? He may as well have been singing in Sanskrit. He was hoarse, unaware, and far out of tune, yet all around him were the gray-painted props, which he had painted red and green, and which he lit with brilliant lights. A veteran of combat and Parkinson's, who wanted to keep the tree set up year-round. When she said goodbye at the open casket viewing, mom touched his cheek and said, "You did it, Johnny." Somehow you knew exactly what she meant.

## About Fred Nolan

Fred Nolan is a speculative fiction writer from
Texas.

# Desert Skin
(E.K. Lloyd-Williams)

Look for the skin-suit in the fifth-wheel.

The message came in much the same manner as the countless others before it. Never once had Isaiah Jackson worked out how the Ghost delivered them; they simply appeared. The letters were not inked, but burned into the paper. Faint tendrils of smoke curled into themselves in the purple desert air, wafting through the turned-down windows of a 1987 Ford Ranger. A new message for a new day.

It was Isaiah's habit to begin his days in the truck, perched on an outcropping of rock overlooking the smallest portion of the New Mexico desert. Facing due east, he would measure the changes in the sun's rising, calculating its position in the evening's setting. He had lived in this desert, off and on, for nearly forty years. He still did not know why the mornings were purple. Always purple. Not the royal purple so many vied for, either. Lavender mornings heralded a good day; plum was the harbinger of the bad days.

Much like the morning's pastel light, the message from the Ghost was something cryptic. What skin-suit, and in which fifth-wheel? If the Ghost were present, it would chide Isaiah for a simpleton.

While the sergeant would not call himself a keen and penetrating mind, Isaiah was more than spoiled for choice in terms of possible definitions and addresses. A skin-suit in a fifth-wheel.

Likely as not, the spirit knew of his location. Otherwise, coordinates would have been included in the missive. Whatever fifth-wheel Isaiah was meant to find, it would probably be in the run-down county he had been traipsing for the last month. Given the Ghost's uncanny ability to find people out, it was entirely likely he would see the shelter from this very outcropping.

The nature of the "skin-suit" was another matter altogether.

It was decidedly too much to hope he was looking for some meth-head in green spandex. He could pray his quarry be a more obvious Ed Gein, though Isaiah wasn't entirely sure God liked him all that much. In all his years as a tracker, Isaiah was never granted the easy luck of merely hunting a deranged wannabe. The Army was never so kind as that, and the Ghost hadn't yet been, either. Isaiah consistently got the grittiest work. The difference between dirty work for the Army and dirty work for the Ghost was the blind eye cast over the ugly bits. Often enough, the Ghost had made the ugly bits worse.

Ugly histories make ugly futures, Isaiah Jackson thought. He had a hunch he knew what skin-suit was supposed to mean. The pit in his stomach which opened up at the thought kept Isaiah rooted to the Ranger's squashed seat. His eyes grew ever wider as the possibility sank in, and suddenly the lavender morning seemed less mysterious and more like God's effort to reassure his creation, this story would have a happy ending. Happier than some, anyway.

Taking a deep breath and muttering a small prayer, Isaiah reassessed the task. His first hurdle was in locating the fifth-wheel. In the whole of New Mexico, it might well have been the official state residence. The fact that the Ghost sent his missive in the morning, without co-ordinates, indicated the fifth-wheel would be somewhere close. The greater county had to be ruled out on that account. The plastic-and-tin hovel was bound to be somewhere around town.

In this unique little New Mexican oasis, that would leave about twenty-seven possible options.

Unless the soldier wanted to visit them all, he would need to pare down the list with specifics. For such an endeavor, he wouldn't require assistance, but to say it would not help might be a lie. Isaiah had one friend in this desolate desert, and they happened to have chilled interactions. It may have been a wariness inspired by Isaiah's choice to join the Army, and thus strain a childhood bond. More likely it was that Isaiah visited Henry on the reservation much more than the natives liked, and no amount of threats or cold shoulders could put the white man off.

Whatever the reason, the Indian would meet the Soldier. There would be no whiskey.

Henry was waiting in his preferred booth when Isaiah entered the diner off the dusted road. His cup of coffee steamed weakly; his steak and eggs would not be far behind. Isaiah crossed to him, smiling wryly when he saw the weak beer.

"How did you know I was buying?"

"Simple enough," said Henry. "Because I knew I wasn't."

"Are you short on cash?" asked Isaiah. "Do you need twenty bucks?"

Henry hid his smile behind the rim of his cup. "That joke wasn't funny the first time."

"I'll put it in your tip jar," Isaiah whispered. "Spare your dignity."

"You would, you under-cooked Dublin pastie," Henry retorted, with only a touch of a sneer. "You gonna pin it to a blanket, too?"

Isaiah suppressed a snort. "I'm Scottish, you racist jerk," he said through a chuckle, "but I do have a blanket in my truck, just for occasions with you, Henry."

"Did you ask me to breakfast just to make racist jokes, asshole?"

"No," said Isaiah, "it's complimentary. I do appreciate you coming, though."

"I wouldn't turn down a free meal," Henry replied. "Why are we here, anyway? We just had dinner last week. You're two weeks ahead of schedule."

Isaiah took a swig of the beer. "A friend of mine got in touch with me," he began.

"You have another friend?" said Henry in surprise.

"Ha," Isaiah retorted. "Yes. Well, no. Not really. More of a, uh, colleague-in-spirit. Anyway, he put me onto something that I'm gonna need some help with, and I thought of you."

Henry frowned, chewing his way through the thick coffee. "What is the nature of the job?" he asked cautiously. They both knew Isaiah would be elsewhere if he could.

The soldier passed the beer bottle between his palms. "An ugly one in a fifth-wheel."

"Well, I'm glad you could narrow it down."

"One we don't talk about," said Isaiah.

Henry narrowed his dark eyes. "No."

"I only need a name."

"You think I have a name?"

"How old could it possibly be?"

Henry leaned in. "Old enough," he hissed. "What are you thinking?"

"That I'm gonna go hunting," said Isaiah coolly. "And I need to know where to set my blind."

Henry fell silent as his plate of steak and eggs arrived. The waitress, having recognized Henry, had gone to the trouble of putting in Isaiah's usual order. She placed the patty melt in front of him with a wink. "Anything else for you, boys?"

They declined, and she moved away. Henry stared at the gray meat and pale eggs for a long moment. "You've lost your white damn mind," he finally muttered.

Isaiah nodded in agreement, biting into the melt. They ate in silence for several minutes, Henry finishing off the eggs and most of the steak in short order. Isaiah bolted down the patty melt, and was still nursing the beer when the Indian leaned back in the booth seat.

"Who is the colleague?" Henry finally asked.

"No one local," Isaiah answered.

Henry's eyebrows shot to the ceiling. "Are you trying to get us both killed?"

"No," said Isaiah evenly, "I'm trying to kill something before it hurts anyone else. And I understand you don't want to talk. We grew up on the same stories, Henry. But the only way to deal with this damn thing is to kill it. Somebody who does what they do is a problem. If the Native boys don't want to deal with it, fine. The white boys will. No skin off your nose. No danger for you. If I succeed, or if I fail, red boys get a win. I'm not asking you to risk your life. I just need information."

He sipped the beer while the Indian thought it over.

The most important thing, in these circumstances, was to wait for the other man to see the sense.

In terms of bravery, Navajo had earned their own reputation. From personal experience, Isaiah knew Henry Weaver to be no form of coward. In the face of such evil as the kind they were taking great care not to openly discuss, white or red, many a man's courage would fail. Isaiah didn't blame him. Were he to fail, his own skin would be the suit.

What irked the soldier was the chronic unwillingness by the native sons to address the wickedness they knew wandered their land. Isaiah didn't blame them for being afraid of it. He did blame them for running away and letting the evil go unchecked. As with most dangers from beyond the veil, the only way to entice them to the edge of the fray was the prospect of a white death. Henry and his family knew the solution; it was passed down from generation to generation. Also handed down was a categorical refusal to act.

"I don't like it," the Indian finally said.

"You don't have to," said Isaiah, "you're not doing it. How many friends?"

"Enough," snarled the other man. "They always have friends."

"Always there?"

"No, but often enough to notice if one of them goes missing."

"Do they run on a cycle?"

Henry shook his head. "That's more than I want to know," he said. "There's one possible place. I've seen an eagle hanging around there. The kind I don't want to get near. It's about fifteen miles off the main highway, down by the arroyo southwest of the water tower. Dirt road, no street name."

Isaiah nodded. "Henry, I need a name."

"I can't give you a name," the other man snapped.

"Because it's old, or because you're worried it'll hear?"

Every one of the creatures had a name. The name they were given before they became death perverted. The only way its name could disappear was for everyone who had ever known it to be dead. Henry took a steadying breath. "Isaiah," he said slowly, "you know good and well we don't like to mess with them. You know why we don't. The pride you whites have in fighting every enemy is the reason so many of you die early. And you will die if you go after that witch. You can tell your colleague to let this one go."

Isaiah stared him down. "I can," he agreed. "I won't."

"You may have no choice," Henry warned. "Why do you think nobody wants to deal with it?"

"I know why, Henry. I'm not excited about the chance of this thing taking my skin, too," Isaiah reassured him. "My colleague got in touch with me about this thing. I didn't call him. So whatever the little bastard is up to, it's not contained here. Not anymore."

What he couldn't explain to Henry was how much he owed the Ghost, and why that unpayable debt meant risking his own life. Isaiah was more than sympathetic to the Indian's misgivings.

When the bill was paid and the two went their separate ways, Isaiah caught a fleeting look of concern as it flashed across Henry's brow.

As he climbed into the Ranger, Isaiah glanced out of the windshield, just over the top of his dashboard. At a distance, roughly five-hundred yards from the diner, a coyote sat perched atop Isaiah's morning outcropping. Careful not to look too closely, the soldier monitored the beast. It
seemed to be watching the vultures circle some miles away. At length, it stood, its full height making the soldier's stomach clench.

Tracking the suit wasn't difficult, strictly speaking. In a town such as this, where everybody knew very nearly everybody, there was no hiding one's occupation, interests, or personality. The exception to this rule was for those living so far outside of town their living and dying became a campfire story, souls aged and nameless. The benefit to existing as a campfire story is that people tend to forget them.

Isaiah, for example, only remembered a particularly applicable campfire story when he stopped by the small hardware store and came face-to-face with a plastic sleeve of popcorn. The following morning, Isaiah sent his own message to Henry: If I'm not dying the next time you see me, for God's sake kill me.

His hunt proved to be one of those times when a passing interest became a necessary pastime.

Isaiah enjoyed the desert sky, and he could track a few constellations as he saw them. The astronomer's need for a wide-open space and a high place to work gave the soldier a perfect excuse to wander the arroyo. With a cheap telescope, a notebook, and a camera old enough to be his mother's third ex-husband, Isaiah drove slowly, following Henry's approximation. There was just enough desert vegetation to make the track difficult, and Isaiah was careful to never let the dead arroyo far from his field of vision.

He camped for several days, driving slowly and refilling the gas tank sparingly. The old engine ate surprisingly little fuel if he kept his speed below 40, and the distance covered was not inconsiderable.

The arroyo covered plenty of ground itself, and tracing as many miles of it as he did, Isaiah found himself admiring the skin-suit for its creative concealment. Eventually, however, the beast gave up the ghost. What better bait for a skin-thief than one's own skin?

The grand moment finally came just after noon on the fifth day of the hunt. Isaiah was just waking up, having spent the night traversing the region, listening to the desert nightlife to find the odd sound out. It was this day, when he woke to Apollo's blinding beam and slowly gathered his bearings, that Isaiah saw the sight he'd been hoping against hope to see.

A familiar sight.

The mangy coyote whose legs weren't quite right, crouched on an outcropping, almost mirroring Isaiah. It had to stand fully upright to really be comfortable, which was usually about the time most people who saw it began to soil themselves.

Isaiah started the engine, letting it idle. He reached over to the passenger side and rifled through the glove box. From the contents he lifted a pack of cigarettes, brand new, and a long silver dagger in a leather sheath. He slid the blade in and out of its protection, coating it in the fine white ash packed into the sheath. He glanced again at the outcropping: the coyote was standing up on its haunches, both front paws a long way off the ground. Isaiah reached for the glove box again, and came out with an M1911.

He released the clip, counted the rounds, and re-inserted it. He made those rounds himself, but he'd never got the chance to use them. Silver bullets capped with a thin filament which would break apart on contact and release yet another dose of white ash into the target.

From the corner of his eye he saw the coyote begin to pace. Even at this distance, it towered.

Following it was out of the question. It could easily catch Isaiah in a trap. Getting it to follow him. . . .

Tearing hell for leather across the desert wouldn't have the ending he wanted. It likely wouldn't even have the beginning. He inched his way slowly forward, bouncing and jollying his way through the dust, back toward the main road. No rush, no sudden movements, no stench of fear. He kept a careful peripheral eye on the skin as he went. It turned in place, watching him go.

Isaiah made his way; the skin followed. He went in what he hoped was an unpredictable, moseying kind of zig-zag pattern. He wasn't expecting any projectiles; it was simply easier to gauge whether or not he had the skin's attention. Would it strike at easy prey?

Eventually, Isaiah came to the shoulder of the main road. When he finally got the front tires on the pavement, the skin was still following. All four tires on the pavement, Isaiah paused in the middle of the stretch of blacktop, twisting to poke his head out of the open window. Only for a single moment, but it was enough to elicit sudden movement.

The sergeant hit the gas, burning rubber and tearing hell for leather down the length. He sent up a prayer of thanks for the straight road. It would make sighting the skin easier as it came running, and minimized the chances of being caught by a sudden turn.

On all lanky fours it kept pace with Isaiah, no matter how he pressed. They went along this way for over a mile, the soldier finding the sense of fun in the little game. The beast seemed to enjoy itself too. It was tempting to think of the distorted look on the monster's face as something akin to a smile.

What creature didn't enjoy showing off, testing its skill and speed?

Fun as it was, it couldn't go on forever. Isaiah rolled the window all the way down, raised the pistol, and fired a single shot. The bullet traveled straight and true, piercing the skin's side and exiting with a burst through the opposite lung. It stumbled over its feet, flopping onto its belly.

Isaiah slammed on the brake and yanked the wheel sharply, coming to a broadside stop in the middle of the blacktop. The lump of flesh struggled to rise. The cap had burst on contact – Isaiah hoped – the white ash would have dusted its internal organs. How long the process was meant to take, the soldier couldn't have said. When it didn't die after several minutes, he sighed in disappointment. "Might as well ask," he said to himself.

Isaiah climbed out of the truck, the dagger in hand. The pistol was on his hip, but if the thing was weak enough, he could put it out of its misery with an old-fashioned head-cutting. Approaching on foot and alone had never been the soldier's favorite, on any battlefield. Even for the chance to watch this particular beast die, he'd have much preferred to keep his distance. Still, the old training had kicked in. In truth, it had never left. Why else would a man return to the isolation of the desert? Why else would he find it so difficult to fit in?

The civilian world had been unbearable when Isaiah returned from Army life. It wasn't until the Ghost found him that the sergeant began to be frustrated when so many of his company brothers ended up eating bullets. But for the work, he'd have gone the same way, he knew that. He couldn't fathom why they didn't know it. Even if it killed him, Isaiah was determined to never go back to that vapid way of life.

Life without a mission. Without purpose. Endless Costco trips, bar tabs, and electric bills, a mobius strip of misery. At least here, now, with this skin before him, Isaiah's life and work, the years of training, blood, and sweat – all of it meant something. Belonged to something real.

The skin was writhing, making sounds so far from human, it was hard to believe the creature had once occupied such a form. It had returned to its human shape in agony, and the drawn and sunken face fixed Isaiah with a look of pure hatred. The mouth wanted to utter a curse, but the ash dissolving its insides made this quite impossible.

Not willing to risk the viability of a stop-start method of cursing, Isaiah crouched beside the monster, pulled the silver dagger from its sheath, and plunged the ash-coated blade into its heart. It was in this final moment of execution that the skin threw a handful of dust in Isaiah's face.

Isaiah jerked away, the dagger's handle still firmly in his grip as the dust coated his mouth and nose. The movement was enough to twist the dagger. He felt the blade cut through the muscle of the heart, felt the warm spray of blood as it erupted from the skin's mouth and coated his hand and arm.

Isaiah coughed and gagged, yanking the dagger from the body. The effects of the dust would be felt in short order, and he couldn't leave before this particular job was done.

It wasn't easy work, but taking a head never was. By the time he had severed spine and sinew, Isaiah was shaking. Heavy labor did nothing to help his situation, but it needed to be done. Even with the skin dead and food for the buzzards, Isaiah would need help, and quickly. If he could make it to Henry and Sidda's, he might find the help he needed. There was no question of whether or not Henry knew someone, but whether Henry would let him die.

Driving to Henry's presented a number of greater dangers than pursuing the skin. The time it had taken to cut off the beast's head had given the powder its chance to begin working. This meant weaker reflexes for Isaiah, and more than a few close calls as he approached the canyon drive along his friend's home. Several instances occurred in which he very nearly went over the canyon wall. As slowly as he would die, Isaiah's strength was rapidly depleting.

He finally found the place, a single-story home sprawled out beneath the desert sun. Henry's truck was in the dirt yard; Sidda's outline was just visible in the front-facing kitchen window. Isaiah, with great effort pushed the truck door open, and fell out of the driver's seat. He saw Sidda's shape moving, though which direction was unclear. The sergeant did not possess the strength to call out, and could only hope she would see his empty vehicle.

It may have been a few minutes, or perhaps several hours, Isaiah didn't bother knowing. In due course, the front door opened, and Henry's light footsteps came rushing toward the soldier's ear.

"Isaiah!" he heard. "Isaiah, you didn't!"

The soldier opened his eyes. "I don't know it was the one," he coughed, "but I got a one."

Isaiah was dragged into the house, because Henry had never treated him with any particular care.

Whatever instructions he gave Sidda, Henry's words were unintelligible to Isaiah. Shaking, shivering, sweating bullets, all the man could focus on was the low burn licking at the edges of his nerves.

These would all give way in short order, and he would begin to turn gray, rotting from the inside out.

If Henry called the medicine man, or if he didn't, there was nothing for Isaiah to do. The only thing he was capable of, for the foreseeable future, was to lay on the bit of floor Henry allotted him, and wait for one inevitability or another.

Time passed from indeterminate to unknowable. Isaiah felt prodding and pulling. Once, he became vaguely aware of being lifted, though to where he could not say. What came after was a guess at best. Thirst took hold of him, though no water was given. Visions came and went, varying in degrees of horror. It may have been a dream in which he saw the other skins collecting the corpse of their fallen brother. Without a head they could not revive him, and so a pyre was built and the body destroyed by fire.

Eventually, hacking and wheezing, Isaiah was restored to consciousness. In a small earthen dwelling, blocked from all but the smallest shivers of determined light, he lay on a thin pallet. As his senses returned, he found himself prone, layered with blankets, breathing in vapors and smoke. The herbs he had once been able to name, the wood so familiar it might have been his father's voice.

Isaiah found he could breathe again.

"You went above and beyond," said a familiar voice, high and rasping. "In more ways than one."

Isaiah turned his head carefully toward the source of the sound. The long, narrow silhouette was a strange sort of comfort. "Oh, the medicine man is not gonna like you."

"He is wary," the Ghost admitted, "but the favor I have done his community is inarguable. Your role in that was instrumental."

"Was it the right one?" Isaiah wheezed through another cough.

"No," said the Ghost, "but he was dealt with all the same."

Isaiah tried to stare at the ceiling of the little hut. He couldn't open his eyes completely for the burning. At length, he understood. "You needed to draw them out."

"I did."

"Who went with you?"

"A hit-man I picked up in Malibu. I would have preferred to have the both of you, but Wakeman acquitted himself. None survived."

Isaiah managed a weak nod. "Good."

"I was rather peeved, I must say," the Ghost went on.

"Why?"

"Your bullet worked well enough," said the spirit. "Why didn't you just shoot him in the heart?"

Isaiah's tired mind thought it over. "If I had the habit of thinking things through, I wouldn't have joined the Army."

The Ghost let out his strange laugh. "Fair enough, Isaiah Jackson. You have survived another fight, thanks in no small part to your friend. I fear, though, it may be the last favor he ever does you."

"Ah," the soldier sighed, "I don't blame him. Why did you need me for this? You could have hunted those animals down on your own. I've seen you do it."

The Ghost did not answer for some time, and when Isaiah began to think he had gone, the spirit finally said: "There are jobs for spirits, and jobs for men. This was the job for men. You did it adequately."

These were his parting words, and Isaiah Jackson chuckled to himself. Feeling the fatigue of his inert battle, the soldier closed his eyes once again. He would be permitted to sleep another day before he was told to go. His association with Ghost now being known, he would have to move on.

This rundown county of New Mexico was no longer open to the soldier.

Perhaps his fortune would be found in Appalachia. Or in the hills of Georgia. Even the bones of the Sierra Nevadas were open to him now. As he drifted off, he let himself wonder what other battles the Ghost deemed for men. Isaiah considered the Dogman rumored to haunt the backwoods of Tennessee. That would make a worthy cause, he thought. A true battle of man against beast.

## About E.K. Lloyd-Williams

E.K. Lloyd-Williams enjoys cryptids and conspiracy theories. Desert Skin is an endeavor inspired by the former, while the character of The Ghost is inspired by the latter. Isaiah Jackson, like all soldiers, is The Ghost's chosen tool for the particular situation described in the story.

As soldiers coming back from war will say themselves, readjusting to civilian life is extraordinarily difficult. They don't just miss the camaraderie of brother warriors, they often miss the war itself. War isn't only violence; it is tactics and strategy, missions and debriefings. There is always another mission, always another plan, always something greater than the individual which the men all work to achieve. To become a civilian is to give that up, to become consumed by the pettiness of day-to-day living. Veteran suicides aren't only caused by PTSD.

It seems likely, therefore, that a soldier such as Isaiah Jackson would have no thought about committing himself to The Ghost and the dangers of pursuing mythical monsters. It's become fashionable to talk about mental health when soldiers are cycled into civilians; for the good of their mental health, veterans ought to be given monsters to hunt and fight.

E.K. Lloyd-Williams has published two other novels. *How to Cure* (2020), the first in a trilogy, and *At the Hands of the Laughing Man* (2023), which is meant to serve as an exhibit in the argument that Rushed Writing is Poor Writing. E.K. also posts to Substack under the nomme de plume Draeg the Writer. Her next novel, *Vampire Bite*, will follow *How to Cure*, and is anticipated for release in 2025.

# A Battle That Never Was
### (Berthold Gambrel)

Crashing and lurching through the mud, the transport groaned in protest as it cleared another hill. Through the narrow slit of window beside which I had managed to squeeze myself, I could see that the night was clear. The moonlight threw a silvery, ghostly glow over the barren terrain, churned already into a sprawling wasteland by artillery. Here and there, the skeletal arms of leafless trees cast eerie twisting shadows over the silver-grayness. Otherwise, all was desolate.

I leaned back from the unnerving sight, and turned my gaze to the more pleasant interior of our vehicle. Wallace and Monroe were playing a game of dice on the floor in front of us; the others huddled around to see and cheer them on. Harrison beside me had fallen asleep; no surprise, given how much rum I'd seen him drink earlier in the day. His head lolled to one side, and I shoved him in the other direction before his helmet could collide with mine.

We had all landed at the port not five standard hours before, then handed rifles and rucksacks and loaded into the squat, boxy gray monstrosity that now rattled over the corpse of what had perhaps once been a vibrant meadow.

We were nervous, and frightened, and excited all at once. The prospect of seeing battle at last after the last six months of endless drilling thrilled us, creating a atmosphere of unique energy into the whole transport room. Every word that was spoken, every look exchanged, every throw of the dice, seem to have to it a heightened sense of reality, as each of our minds buzzed with the imminent presence of death.

At last, the sergeant called for lights out. The word went round that we would not see the front till morning, although no sooner had the lights extinguished and we all retired to our bunks then a distant rumble could be heard. At first, we took it for thunder; but soon realized it was the constant barrage of heavy shells being launched, rockets exploding into the entrenchments we were approaching.

I doubt if any of us slept, but all pretended to, each alone with his thoughts on the eve of our first battle. I clutched my unloaded rifle close and tried to visualize myself in combat, victoriously standing over my defeated foes, to block out any intruding images of other possibilities.

I don't know how long I lay there, but eventually I must have drifted off, though I do not recall becoming aware of waking up. The next thing I knew, the endless metal growl of the leviathan transport died suddenly, and all grew quite silent, and I was now uncomfortably aware of my own breathing, and the beating of my heart, as well as that of my fellows.

Thin rays of moons' light still seeped in through the slitted aperture, and from its steadiness and the lack of any vibrations through the bunk, I was suddenly conscious that we were not moving. The stillness began to unnerve me. For some time, I lay there listening, waiting, expecting to hear voices, or to see someone come to rouse us, or some other indication as to what was happening. But nothing happened.

Finally, I decided to stand and stretch my legs. Carefully making my way over the huddled forms of my sleeping comrades, I reached the hatch that led to the exterior. I slowly turned the heavy metal wheel to open it, and stepped outside into the cool night air.

I realized almost immediately that it was inexcusably foolish of me to exit without even taking my rifle. My only weapon was the hunting knife strapped to my thigh, which would be of little use against an enemy attack. I thought I should return to my blanket and go back to sleep. Yet my body did not wish to obey. Mechanically, I stepped off the narrow metal walkway and hopped down to the muddy ground.

The artillery's distant roar had subsided, and now the night was still. The quiet noises of the nocturnal birds and insects squeaked and chirped in the darkness. It was pleasant, all in all, except for the indescribable but visceral feeling of anticipation that seemed thick in the air itself. Of course, this may have been merely my imagination.

Something faint at the edge of my gaze caught my eye. It was a sensation of something moving, though I could not say for certain that anything was actually there. A feeling more than an actual observation; yet I turned automatically in that direction.

As my eyes adjusted to the light, I perceived that our transport was stopped on the floor of a small depression in the landscape, with gentle hills rolling up on every side. We were traveling north, and turning to my right, I perceived the feeling of motion had come from the east.

Presently, I saw at the top of one of the hills a gently flickering light, glowing softly, warmly; as of a fire.

There was little reason to think it would be an encampment, and in any case, any base camp would use a generator and an electric light. More than likely, I supposed, this was a fire lit by a stray shell that would soon enough burn itself out.

I cannot explain rationally why I chose to move towards the light any more than a moth could.

My actions that night are susceptible of no logical description. All I can do is report them. In any case, begin

walking towards it is what I did, heedless of any regulation
or even basic good sense.

The chirping and warbling of the night creatures
died away then, and I was aware as I walked of an eerie
stillness settling upon me. There was the same muffled,
gauzy feeling as one gets in a thick fog at night. And yet,
there was no fog. Indeed, the night was exceptionally
clear. Yet the impression of being unable to see or hear
was extremely strong.

As I walked towards the light, I began to mentally
sing, or perhaps silently mouth, the lyrics to the
melancholy old tune *I Left My Love Beneath The Purple
Sun*. At the time, I had no idea why I thought of that
maudlin ballad, but now, thinking back I wonder if it was
because our commandant told us a story about a company
that sang it as they marched directly into an enemy
legion's guns, the last of them still belting it out to the very
end as the shells cut him
down.

In any case, I was still mindlessly muttering the
words to myself as I ascended the hill and saw that the
light was that of a signal fire, lit in a small stone structure,
not far from which sat a low, squat cabin, also made of
stone. It was a small abode, and must have contained only
one or at most two rooms. It was windowless, with a
wooden door and a chimney as the only notable features.
From the chimney I could see a little smoke emerging, and
I thought I heard a sort of singing or chanting from
within, suggesting the building was occupied.

This suspicion was confirmed when the door
creaked slightly open, and the firelight from within seeped
out into the night. Cautiously, I stepped forward and
nudged the door till it swung further open, allowing me to
see within.

The cabin's interior was thick with smoke—a sickly sweet smell which I did not like. It reminded me of something, though I am not sure exactly what. The room was furnished with only a few chairs and a long slab of stone which served as a table, set a little ways out from the fireplace.

At this table was seated a figure, clad in a flowing, thin robe of the most remarkable material I had ever seen. A very warm gold, it glittered and glistened in the firelight, shifting about slowly, as the cloaked head swiveled toward me. In the gloom, I could not see the face concealed beneath the cowl, but could feel the gaze of eyes upon me.

"Be seated," said the figure in a low, female-sounding voice.

I obeyed automatically, and placed myself in the chair opposite the speaker. I felt a vague sense of terror, and yet at a curious remove, as though it was not happening to me but to someone else.

Suddenly, I became aware that the flat stone surface before me had changed, almost melted, into a picture, as if viewed from bird flying above, of a great war-torn battlefield. The dead and dying lay in gruesome oozing heaps amid burnt-out wreckage, smoke, and debris. Spent shells and discarded weapons crisscrossed the soot-blackened ground. The scene was one of unutterable horror, and I felt now recalled to myself, and looked away in shock and disgust.

"Come, come!" barked the figure in the cloak. "Can it be that you equip yourself for war, bedeck thyself in martial array, and yet, when confronted with the inevitable consequences of the same, shrink away in terror?"

I looked toward the hooded face, trying to find eyes that I could meet evenly. But in the shadows there were none, only the faint hint of a weathered jaw and a thin, scowling mouth.

"I'm not afraid, if that's what you mean," I replied as firmly as I could.

"Ach, the false bravado of a child," came the croaked reply. "What you think is bravery is only denial of the truth. A man's heart should ne'er be void of fear, but instead accepting of it. Fear is only consciousness of death, and death is aught of which ye be assured."

I stared back, silently, at this unnerving, disturbing, inexplicable being. I was now sure that I must be dreaming. This was less comforting than you might think.

But she continued, "You have yet to fight your war, but already you must accept that it may end with your demise."

"I'm a soldier. Such are the risks we take," I answered, some of my old confidence returning.

A faint chuckle emanated from beneath the hood, something infinitely more terrifying than I could have imagined. Now, she drew back her hood a little, and a weathered, lined face stared back at me, a hard, almost cruel, face etched with the impression of a thousand horrors. Despite myself, I flinched and averted my gaze.

"Then why not step outside, and see it for yourself?" she croaked.

A long, thin arm lifted from the figure's lap and from within the folds of the glittering fabric emerged a withered, bony hand, deathly pale and spotted with ugly purplish blotches. A horribly twisted finger pointed toward the door. I turned, and saw it swing slowly open, its rusted hinges squealing as it did so.

I rose from my seat, again with the horrible feeling of being somehow externally controlled, and walked to the now-open doorway.

It was still night when I emerged, but not the quiet, cool evening which it had been. The air was thick with the hot, acrid smell of smoke, and the roar of artillery and small arms fire was nearly deafening. How, I wondered, could I not have heard it in the small cabin? I reminded myself again that this was a dream, that it must be a dream.

I walked slowly down the hill, my eyes adjusting to the flickering orange light of the omnipresent fires, gradually coming to the awful realization that the ground all around me was littered with corpses, and not only corpses but the horribly mangled bodies of dying men, pleading, screaming, wailing, and sobbing in agony.

It's only a dream, I reminded myself, praying fervently that I would soon wake, back inside the troop transport.

Suddenly, a hand shot out from amid the bloody heaps and grabbed at my leg. I looked down and saw Wallace staring up at me, his face bloodied and torn, and a look of anguish in his eyes. He screamed for water, and I quickly drew out my canteen and handed it to him, watching as he eagerly gulped, water mixing with blood on his lips.

Soon, more of the piles of wounded around me began to moan and flail for a drink as well, and I felt torn between my pity for the suffering men and a need to keep moving, and so began to shove my way through the thicket of bloody clutching hands and awful screaming disfigured bodies around me. The piercing scent of blood and charred flesh seared at my nostrils, and the oppressive heat caused me to break into a sweat, the moisture running down my brow and burning my eyes till I could not see. Now I felt only the sensation of being dragged down, down into the dark mass of death...

******

I awoke from the dream aboard the transport again. Never had I ever thought I would be glad to see those drab metal walls and hear that monotonous mechanical thudding again, but now it was like listening to a soft serenade in a favorite lounge! I opened my eyes slowly, letting them gradually focus on the dimly lit room around me.

"Poor fellow," I heard someone say somewhere nearby.

I looked around to see a man in a medic uniform standing over me. He was writing some notes on a clipboard and seemed to have directed this comment at a sergeant who was standing at his side.

"Looks like he's waking up now, though," the other commented, with a glance towards me.

"Y-yes," I said shakily, and attempted to rise, only to feel my legs wobble beneath me and quickly abandoned the effort.

I sank back down to the bed and realized I was not in exactly the same part of the transport as before. This section was a labyrinth of small cubicles or compartments, unlike the more open area. *What had happened to everyone else?*

"He's still a bit out of it," the medic said.

The sergeant crouched down beside me. "How are you feeling, private?" he asked, putting a hand on my shoulder.

I rubbed my brow in confusion.

"What's going on...?" I asked. "We were just about to go into battle."

The sergeant gave me a weak, joyless smile. "We've been in a battle, son. You were in the thick of it. I think you just don't want to remember it."

"But that, that's..." I stammered, looking around wildly. I realized now the other compartments around me held wounded men, each missing limbs or horribly disfigured.

"You held your post against a whole advancing enemy battalion. You'll be getting medals for what you did out there," he continued in a tone of reassurance.

There had to be some kind of mistake. I had never been in combat. I had never seen an enemy soldier.

"Look," I said, with as much conviction as I could manage, "where are Wallace and Monroe? Or Harrison? We're in the same unit—"

"They didn't make it," he replied grimly.

The truth of his words hit me like a punch in the jaw. Somehow, although I didn't want to admit it, I could feel it. I didn't reply. I found myself envisioning that awful scene I had dreamt. Or witnessed? Or...?

"We should have him talk to the counselor," the medic said. "He needs someone who is trained to talk about these things. I'll go find her."

The sergeant said nothing, but nodded and stood up. The medic turned and walked away from the small compartment, and the other man followed behind him, leaving me to lie back and look at the ceiling. The shadeless electric bulbs flickered and swung as the transport bounced up and down, casting weird dancing shadows on the wall.

Had I been in combat? As assured as I was of the death of my comrades, I was nowhere near as convinced that I had taken part in any fighting. I had spoken to veterans who told me they never forgot their first combat, no matter how much they might have wished to do so. Then again, the horror of my dream was so vivid, so fresh... where had my mind drawn those images, if not the firsthand experience of battle?

I heard the voice of the medic again, coming back in the direction of my compartment.

"Yes, I think you'll recognize all the symptoms," he was saying, and then paused. Whomever he was talking to said something in reply, but I couldn't make it out.

"Oh, you know him, then? I see. Well, that should help."

He entered my view and gestured to his companion. "This is our counselor; she will be able to help you with processing everything you went through."

He said something more at this point, but I didn't hear what it was. I was too transfixed with shock at what I saw. For the face of the woman at his side was none other than that of the horrible aged creature in the cloak.

## About Berthold Gambrel

The idea for my story came from... well, to tell you the truth, I don't know where it came from. I wrote it using a technique I learned about from none other than Mark Paxson himself, which is:  start writing and see what happens. I had no idea where it would go when I started writing it, which is a first for me when embarking on a writing project. Doing this was a fun experiment.

I've written two novels, two more novellas or long short stories, all of which you can find on Amazon. I also write a blog, which these days consists mostly of book reviews and can be found at ruinedchapel.com